WITHDRAWN

IN A STRANGE ROOM

Damon Galgut

IN A STRANGE ROOM
THREE JOURNEYS

Europa
editions

Europa Editions
116 East 16th Street
New York, N.Y. 10003
www.europaeditions.com
info@europaeditions.com

Library of Congress Cataloging in Publication Data is available
ISBN 978-1-60945-011-3

Galgut, Damon
In a Strange Room

Book design by Emanuele Ragnisco
www.mekkanografici.com
Cover photo © Renaud Visage/Getty Images

Prepress by Grafica Punto Print – Rome

Printed in Canada

CONTENTS

IN A STRANGE ROOM

He Has No House
—VOJISLAV JAKIĆ

ONE

THE FOLLOWER

I t happens like this. He sets out in the afternoon on the track that has been shown to him and soon he leaves the little town behind. In an hour or so he is among low hills covered by olive trees and grey stones, from which there is a view out over a plain that gradually descends to the sea. He is intensely happy, which is possible for him when he is walking and alone.

As the road rises and falls there are moments when he can see far ahead and other moments when he can see nothing at all. He keeps looking out for other people, but the huge landscape seems to be completely deserted. The only sign of human beings is the occasional house, tiny and distant, and the fact of the road itself.

Then at some point, as he comes to the crest of a hill, he becomes aware of another figure far away. It could be male or female, it could be any age, it could be travelling in either direction, towards him or away. He watches until the road dips out of sight, and when he comes to the top of the next rise the figure is clearer, coming towards him. Now they are watching each other, while pretending they are not.

When they draw even they stop. The figure is a man about his own age, dressed entirely in black. Black pants and shirt, black boots. Even his rucksack is black. What the first man is wearing I don't know, I forget.

They nod hello, they smile.

Where have you come from.

Mycenae. He points back over his shoulder. And you.

The man in black also points, vaguely, into the distance behind him. And where are you going to. He has an accent the first man cannot place, Scandinavian maybe, or German.

To the ruins.

I thought the ruins were that way.

Yes. Not those ruins, I've seen them.

There are other ruins.

Yes.

How far.

I think ten kilometres. That's what I was told.

He nods. He has a sullen sort of beauty, with long silky hair that falls around his shoulders. He is smiling, though there is nothing to smile at. And where do you come from.

South Africa. And you.

I am from Germany. Where are you staying in Mycenae.

At the youth hostel.

There are a lot of people.

I'm the only one there. Are you staying.

He shakes his head, the long tresses lift and float. I am taking the train tonight. To Athens.

They have conducted this conversation with a curious formality, the width of the road between them, and yet there is something in the way they relate that is not quite intimate, but familiar. As if they have met somewhere before, long ago. But they have not.

Enjoy the ruins, the German man smiles. The South African says that he will. Then they part again with a nod and draw slowly away from each other on the narrow white road, looking back now and then, until they are two tiny and separate points again, rising and falling with the undulations of the land.

He gets to the ruins in the middle of the afternoon. I can't even remember now what they are, the remains of some big but obscure building, there was a fence that had to be climbed, there was a fear of dogs but no dogs appeared, he stumbles around among rocks and pillars and ledges, he tries to imagine how it was but history resists imagining. He sits on the edge of a raised stone floor and stares out unseeingly into the hills around him and now he is thinking of things that happened in the past. Looking back at him through time, I remember him remembering, and I am more present in the scene than he was. But memory has its own distances, in part he is me entirely, in part he is a stranger I am watching.

By the time he comes to himself again, the sun is already low in the sky, the shadows of the mountains are stretched out across the plain. He walks back slowly in the blue coolness. The stars are seeding themselves in bright beds overhead, the earth is huge and old and black. It's long past suppertime when he arrives at the edge of the little village and goes up the deserted main street, the shops and restaurants shuttered and barred, all the windows unlit, through the open front door of the hostel, up the stairs, through passages, past rooms filled with row after row of unoccupied bunk beds, all dark and cold, nobody visiting at this time of year, to the last and highest room, in the middle of the roof, a white cube fixed to a plane. He is very tired now, and hungry, and wants to sleep.

But inside the room the German is waiting. He is sitting on one of the beds, his hands between his knees, smiling.

Hello.

He goes in and closes the door behind him. What are you doing here.

I missed the train tonight. There is another one in the morning. I decided to wait until then. I asked him to put me in your room.

I see that.

You don't mind.

I'm just surprised, I wasn't expecting, no, I don't mind.

He doesn't mind, but he is also uneasy. He knows that the other man has delayed his journey not because of the train but because of him, because of the conversation they had in the road.

He sits down on his own bed. They smile at each other again.

How long are you here for.

I'm also going in the morning.

Are you going to Athens.

No. The other way. To Sparta.

So you've seen Mycenae already.

I've been here two days.

Ah.

There is a silence now in which neither of them moves.

I might stay another day. I'm not in a rush. I like this place.

The German considers. I thought I might also. I haven't seen Mycenae.

You should see it.

So you are staying.

Yes.

Yes. Then I am staying also. For a day.

It feels as if they've agreed to something more than this practical arrangement, but what exactly isn't clear. It is late and cold and the little room is raw and ugly in the fluorescent light.

In a short while the South African gets into his sleeping bag. He is shy and though he would normally undress he doesn't do so tonight. He takes off his shoes and his watch and his two copper bracelets and gets in and lies on his back. He can see the metal slats of the bunk above him and disconnected images from the day come back to him, the ruins, the road, the gnarled shapes of the olive trees.

The German also readies himself for bed. He lays out his sleeping bag on the bunk he's sitting on. Of course his sleeping bag is black.

He unlaces his boots and takes them off, setting them side by side on the floor. Perhaps he too would normally undress but he doesn't tonight, there is no way to know what he would normally do. He doesn't wear a watch. In his black socks he goes to the door to switch off the light, then goes softly back to his bed and climbs in. He takes a few moments to settle.

The South African says something.

I can't hear you.

What is your name.

Reiner. And you.

I'm Damon.

Damon. Good night.

Good night, Reiner.

Good night.

When he wakes up the next day the other bed is empty and the hissing of water comes from the shower next door. He gets up and goes outside, onto the roof. The air is freezing and brilliant and clear. He crosses to the edge and sits down on the parapet, with all the other roofs in the town below him, the main street running from west to east, the tiny shapes of horses in a field. He is very far away from home.

Reiner comes out onto the roof, drying his long hair with a towel. He is wearing the same black pants from yesterday, but no shirt, his body is brown and hard, perfectly proportioned. He knows that he is beautiful and somehow this makes him ugly. He stands in the sun, drying himself, and then also crosses over to sit on the parapet. The towel is slung around his neck, his skin is full of goose-bumps from the cold, beads of water shine like metal in the coarse hair on his chest.

What do you want to do today.

What about these ruins.

They go to the ruins. He has already seen them, he spent several hours there yesterday, but now he looks at the thick walls and foundations and fortifications and tall tombs through the eyes of Reiner, whose expression doesn't change as he walks around from one level to the next at the same unvarying pace, his long body perfectly upright. He sits on a rock to wait and Reiner comes to crouch down nearby. Tell me about this place, he says.

I don't know much about the facts, I'm mostly interested in the mythology.

Tell me that then.

He tells what he remembers, how the lonely woman waited
for her husband to return from the long war at Troy, incubat-
ing revenge out of grief over her murdered daughter, nothing
fuels revenge as grief does, a lesson history teaches over and
over, joining her rage with that of her lover who has his own
griefs to avenge, till the day that Agamemnon comes back,
bringing with him his captive concubine, the prophetess, who
sees what the future holds but can do nothing to prevent it. He
walks in over the bright tapestries that his wife has spread
before him, dragging ten years of siege behind him in his wake,
Cassandra follows, both of them are slaughtered inside. He is
struck down in his bath, for some reason this single image is
the one that stays most vivid and real, the huge man felled by
axes, spouting blood, collapsing naked into the scarlet water,
why is violence always so easy to imagine but tenderness stays
locked in words for me. Already in the ending of this story the
next cycle of grief and revenge is inevitable, that is to say the
following story must begin. And is this true, Reiner says. What
do you mean by that. I mean did it happen. No, no, this is the
myth, but myth always has some fact in it. And what is the fact
here. I don't know, this place exists, for a long time people
thought it didn't, that's a fact to start with. I'm not much
interested in myths, Reiner says, let's climb up there.

He means the mountain behind the ruins.

Up there.

Yes.

Why.

Because, he says. He is smiling again, there is a peculiar glint in his eye, some kind of challenge has been issued that it would be failure to refuse.

They start to climb. On the lower slope there is a ploughed field they walk carefully around, then the mountain goes up steeply, they pick their way through undergrowth and pull themselves through branches. The higher they go the more jumbled and dangerous the rocks become. After an hour or so they have come out on a lower shoulder of the mountain with its tall peak looming overhead, but he doesn't want to go further than this. Here, he says. Here, Reiner says, looking up, have you had enough. Yes. There is a moment before the answer comes, okay, and when they settle themselves on a rock the German has a strange sardonic look on his face.

Now the ruins are far below and the two or three other people in them are as tiny as toys. The sun is already high and despite the time of year the day is warm. Reiner takes his shirt off and bares again that flat belly with its gun-powder trail of dark hair leading down, down. What are you doing in Greece, he says.

Me. Just travelling around. Just looking.

Looking at what.

I don't know.

How long have you been travelling for.

A few months.

Where have you been.

I started in England. France, Italy, Greece, Turkey, now I'm back in Greece. I don't know where I'm going from here.

There is a silence while the German studies him and he looks away, down into the valley, out across the plain to the distant blue mountains, there is a question behind these questions that he doesn't want to answer.

And you.

I have come here to think.

To think.

Yes, I have a problem at home. I wanted to come and walk for a few weeks and think.

Reiner says this and then closes his eyes. He will not speak either, but in him silence is power. Unlike me, unlike me. I also take my shirt off, to bask in the warm sun. Then, he doesn't know why, he doesn't stop, he takes his shoes and socks off, his pants, he is in his underpants on the rock, the air is not warm any more. Both of them understand that he is in some way offering himself, thin and pale and edible on the grey stone. He also closes his eyes.

When he opens them again Reiner is busy putting on his shirt. His expression remains unchanged, he gives nothing away. It's lunchtime, he says, I want to go down.

T he next memory that comes is of evening and somehow it's an inversion of that morning, he is sitting on the parapet again while the last light is fading from the sky, Reiner is in the shower again, the noise of the water carries. Then it stops. A little later he comes out, shirtless again, the towel around his neck, and crosses to sit beside him on the low wall. There is silence for a while and then, as if answering a question that has just been put to him, Reiner says softly that he has come here to think about a woman.

The sun has gone now, the first stars are showing through.

A woman.

Yes. There is this woman in Berlin. She wants to marry me. I don't want to get married, but she won't see me any more if I don't marry her.

This is your problem.

Yes.

And have you decided.

Not yet. But I don't think I will get married.

The town is built on a slope that continues gently downward for a kilometre or two and then flattens into the plain that runs on to the sea. Where the plain begins is the railway line that brought him here and that will take him away tomorrow and on which, at this moment, a train is distantly passing, its carriages lit from inside by a yellow glow. He watches the train pass. I'm also here because of someone else, he says. But I'm not trying to decide, just to forget.

I thought so.

This person is not a woman.

Reiner makes a gesture on the air, as if he is throwing something away. A man or a woman, he says, it makes no difference to me.

This seems to mean one thing, but may mean another. Later that night in the little room, when they are preparing for bed, he strips down to his underpants, as he did earlier in the day on the rock, then rolls quickly into his sleeping bag. It is very cold tonight. Reiner takes a long time to get ready, folding up his shirt and socks and putting them into his bag. Then he takes off his pants. He does this with a certain sense of ceremony, standing in the centre of the room, folding the pants. Then in his underwear, which isn't black, he crosses to the other bed, the one in which I am lying, and sits down on the edge. Would you like some, he says, holding out an apple, I found this in my bag. The two of them pass it between them, solemnly biting and chewing, the one lying propped up on an elbow, the other sitting with his knees drawn up, all it will take is a tiny movement from one of them, a hand extended, or the edge of the sleeping bag lifted, would you like to get in, but neither makes the move, one is too scared and the other too proud, then the apple is finished, the moment is past, Reiner gets up, rubbing his shoulders, it's cold in here, he goes back to his own bed.

The light is still on. After a moment he gets up to put it off. Then he crosses the dark room to the other bed and sits down next to Reiner. He doesn't have an apple to offer and both of them wait in silence, breathing, for the gesture that neither of them will make, then he gets up and goes back to his own bed. He finds that he is trembling.

In the morning they are formal and correct with each other again. They pack their bags. Would you like my address, Reiner says, maybe you will come to Germany one day. He writes it into the little book himself, the tight letters precisely inscribed, then asks, could I have your address too. I don't have an address, I don't have a place, but I'll give you the name of a friend, this he writes down for the other man, then the exchange is complete. They walk together along the main street out of town, down the long slope to the railway station. Their trains are leaving minutes apart, going in different directions. The railway station is a single room and a concrete platform at the edge of the endless green plain, they are the only passengers waiting, a single official behind a dirty window sells them tickets and then comes out himself when the first train appears, to blow his whistle. The South African gets on and goes to the window. Goodbye, he says, I'm glad I met you.

Me too.

Listen.

Yes.

Why do you always wear black.

The German smiles. Because I like it, he says.

The train starts to move.

I will see you again, Reiner says and raises a hand, and then he is disappearing slowly into distance, the solid landscape turning liquid as it pours.

He goes to Sparta, he goes to Pylos. A few days after he leaves Mycenae he is passing through a public square in a town when he sees images of bombs and burning on a television in a café. He goes closer. What is this, he asks some of the people sitting watching. One of them who can speak English tells him that it's war in the Gulf. Everybody has been waiting and waiting for it, now it's happening, it's happening in two places, at another point on the planet and at the same time on the television set.

He watches, but what he sees isn't real to him. Too much travelling and placelessness have put him outside everything, so that history happens elsewhere, it has nothing to do with him. He is only passing through. Maybe horror is felt more easily from home. This is both a redemption and an affliction, he doesn't carry any abstract moral burdens, but their absence is represented for him by the succession of flyblown and featureless rooms he sleeps in, night after night, always changing but somehow always the same room.

The truth is that he is not a traveller by nature, it is a state that has been forced on him by circumstance. He spends most of his time on the move in acute anxiety, which makes everything heightened and vivid. Life becomes a series of tiny threatening details, he feels no connection with anything around him, he's constantly afraid of dying. As a result he is hardly ever happy in the place where he is, something in him is already moving forward to the next place, and yet he is also never going towards something, but always away, away. This is a defect in his nature that travel has turned into a condition.

Twenty years before this, for different reasons, something similar had come over his grandfather. Rooted and sedentary for most of his long life, when his wife died something inside the old man broke irrevocably and he took to the road. He travelled all around the world, to the most distant and unlikely places, fuelled not by wonder or curiosity but grief. Postcards and letters with peculiar stamps and markings arrived in the post-box at home. Sometimes he would phone and his voice would come up, it sounded, from the bottom of the sea, hoarse with the longing to be back again. But he didn't come back. Only much later, when he was very old and exhausted, did he finally return for good, living out his last years in a flat in the back garden behind the house. He wandered around between the flowerbeds, wearing pyjamas at midday, his hair wild and unwashed. By then his mind was going. He couldn't remember where he'd been. All the images and impressions and countries and continents he'd visited had been erased. What you don't remember never happened. As far as he was concerned, he had never travelled anywhere beyond the edges of the lawn. Irascible and mean for much of his life, he was mostly docile now, but still capable of irrational rage. What are you talking about, he screamed at me once, I've never been to Peru, I don't know anything about it, don't talk rubbish to me about Peru.

He leaves Greece two weeks later. He moves around from place to place for a year and a half and then he goes back to South Africa. Nobody knows that he's arrived. He rides in from the airport on the bus, carrying his bag on his knees, looking through the tinted windows at the city he's come back to live in, and there is no way to say how he feels.

Everything has changed while he was away. The white government has capitulated, power has succumbed and altered shape. But at the level on which life is lived nothing looks very different. He gets out at the station and stands in the middle of the moving crowds and tries to think, I am home now, I have come home. But he feels that he is only passing through.

He catches a taxi to the house of a friend, who has got married in his absence. She is happy to see him, but even in her first embrace he senses how much of a stranger he's become. To her, and to himself. He's never been to this house before and he wanders through it, looking at furniture and ornaments and pictures that feel intolerably heavy to him. Then he goes out into the garden and stands in the sun.

His friend comes out to find him. There you are, she says, it's such a coincidence you arrived today, this was in the postbox for you this morning. She gives him a letter which might have fallen from the sky. It comes from Reiner.

They start writing to each other. Every two or three weeks the letters go back and forth. The German is dry and factual, he talks about events in his life from the outside. He went back to Berlin. He didn't get married. He started studying at university, but changed his mind and dropped out. Later he went to Canada, which is where his letters are coming from now, he is on some forestry project somewhere, planting trees.

He tries to imagine him, the dour figure in black with his long silky hair, putting saplings into the ground and tamping down the soil. He can't remember him very well, not the way he looked, what he retains is the feeling that Reiner stirred in him, a sense of uneasiness and excitement. But he wouldn't dare to express this, he senses a reluctance in the other man to talk openly about emotions, to do so is somehow a weakness. But however forthright Reiner seems to be about facts, there are still many details missing in his account of himself, with whom did he live in Berlin, who pays for him to go travelling everywhere, what brought him to Canada to plant trees. Somehow, even when these questions are put to him directly, Reiner manages not to answer.

For his part, he has never withheld emotions, if anything he vents them too freely, at least in letters. Because words are unattached to the world. So it is easy to write to Reiner about how hard he finds it to be back. He can't seem to settle anywhere. He stays with his friend and her husband for a while, but he is an intrusion, an imposition, he knows he has to move on. He takes a room in a house with a student, but he is miserable there, the place is dirty and full of fleas, he doesn't fit in, after a month or two he moves again. He looks after people's houses while they are away, he beds down in spare rooms. Then he moves into a flat owned by an ex-landlady of his, who occupies the three rooms adjacent and below. But this is a mistake. The landlady comes into his flat at all hours, her yapping poodle follows at her heels, she is going through a bad time, she needs to talk, he tries to listen but he is full of unhappiness of his own. He wants to be alone but she won't leave him in peace, the dog sheds hair and hysteria all over his floor. At some point he writes to Reiner, I wish you would come here and take me on a long walk somewhere. A letter comes back, thank you for your invitation, I will be there in December.

D on't meet me at the airport, Reiner tells him, I will find you, there is no need. But he phones the airlines to find out the flight, he borrows a car from friends and is in the arrivals hall an hour before the time. He feels a mixture of anticipation and anxiety. It is two years since they saw each other, he doesn't know how things will be.

When Reiner comes through the door he isn't expecting anybody and so he isn't looking around. I stand a little way back to observe him. His appearance is the same. The glossy brown hair hangs down around his shoulders, he is dressed in black from head to foot, he carries the same black rucksack on his back. With a severe expression he goes over immediately to a row of plastic chairs to rearrange his bag.

I watch for a minute or two, then try to look casual as I stroll over and stand beside him.

Hello.

Reiner looks up. The dark face clears for a moment, then closes over again. Why are you here. I said you should not.

I know. But I wanted to come.

Well.

Hello.

They are unsure of how to greet each other. He opens his arms and the other man accepts the embrace. But not entirely.

Do you not trust me to find my way.

I just wanted to welcome you, that's all. Can I help you with your stuff.

I have just the one bag. I prefer to carry it myself.

He drives Reiner to his place. As they go up the stairs, the land-lady, who is no longer on speaking terms with him, watches through her half-opened door. His flat is almost bare and empty, his few possessions packed into boxes, he will be leaving here at the end of the month. They go out to sit on the balcony, looking down on green trees, the Cape Flats spreading away to the mountains. For the first time he falls silent.

So, Reiner says.

Yes.

I am here.

It's strange.

They look at each other, both smiling. Till now the fact of Reiner's arrival was unreal, he didn't quite believe it would happen, but now they are both in the same place again. They sit out on the balcony, talking. At first they are nervous and awkward with each other, the words don't come easily and are charged with tension when they do. But after only a short while conversation starts to flow, they relax a little, they discover to their relief that they get on well, that they share a certain humour related to an alienation from things. This helps them to like each other again, even if the liking is based on nothing solid as yet, only a vague sense of affinity. It is almost enough.

There is only one bed in his flat, which they have to share. But that night, when the time comes to sleep, Reiner says he doesn't need a mattress.

What do you mean.

He watches while Reiner goes out onto the balcony and starts unpacking his bag. People need too many things, he explains, taking out a sleeping bag and a thin mat. People want to make themselves comfortable. It is not necessary. He unrolls the mat on the balcony and spreads his sleeping bag on top of it. This is all that is necessary. I prefer it. He takes off his shoes and gets into the sleeping bag and zips it up. He lies there, looking at his companion through the dark.

It's impossible to see any expression on his face. Perfect, he says.

Now that Reiner is here he takes the atlas down and they both pore over it anxiously. They are looking for a country full of open space, with few cities. In the time they've spent talking about the trip they have agreed on the sort of conditions ideal for them. Neither of them is looking for lots of people or busy roads or built-up areas. So there is Botswana. There is Namibia. There is Zimbabwe.

And what is this place here.

Lesotho.

What do you know about this place.

He doesn't know much, he's never been there, nor have any of his friends. He knows it's full of mountains and very poor and surrounded entirely by South Africa, but apart from this the country is a mystery to him. They both sit looking at it.

Maybe we should go there.

Maybe we should.

These might not be the words they use, but the decision is as light and unconsidered as this, one moment they don't know where they are going, the next they are off to Lesotho.

They make their way to a government office in town the next day and are given a map, on which all the roads and settlements and altitudes are clearly marked. To me this map looks ideal, but Reiner studies it dubiously.

What's the matter.

Don't you think we should get bigger maps. With more detail. Four or five of them for the whole country.

But what for.

Then we can plan every part of the walk.

But we can plan with this.

But not enough.

They look at each other, this is the first time they're out of step. But the man behind the desk says that he doesn't have more detailed maps anyway, this is the best he can do. It's fine, I say, we'll take it. But later in the day Reiner says, we must look when we get up to Lesotho.

Look for what.

For maps with more detail.

These contradictions are confusing, here is a man who finds a proper bed unnecessary but for whom a perfectly good map is insufficient. The next day Reiner takes himself off to the local library to read up on Lesotho. This is a relief, at least we will know something about where we're going, but when he gets back it turns out he hasn't found out about the history of the country at all. Instead he's researched the climate, the terrain and topography, everything coded into numbers.

Numbers are some form of security for Reiner. When he is offered coffee in the evening he says no, I've had two cups already today, I don't drink more than two cups every twelve hours. When they go walking anywhere he wants to know how many kilometres it is. If he doesn't know, or if he doesn't know exactly, then Reiner looks displeased.

So even in the first few days I become aware of certain differences between them. But there is no time to worry about this. There are still two weeks before they leave and he has a lot to do, he must settle his accounts and put all his things into storage. He is feeling harried and under pressure and in this state he would prefer to be alone. But he is hardly ever alone. Even when he leaves his flat on the most mundane errand Reiner is always with him. He is worn down by the constant presence, like some kind of dark attendant angel, ironic and brooding, his face almost petulant. And Reiner in his turn seems irritated by all these tasks and duties, the requirements of a normal life are beneath him.

Why must you do all these stupid things.

I have to. They have to be done.

Why, Reiner says, smirking.

It is a mystery who attends to all the mundane necessities of Reiner's life at home. When he thinks about it, he knows nothing about Reiner, but if he asks he doesn't get anywhere. He finds out that his parents are deeply religious, but beyond that he has no idea about his family or his background. Though he is genuinely interested, he senses a deep reluctance on the other side to respond.

Once he asks Reiner, what do you do for money.

What do you mean, what do I do.

How do you earn it. Where does it come from.

Money comes. You shouldn't worry about it.

But you have to work for money.

I got paid in Canada. For planting trees.

And before that.

I am a philosopher, Reiner says, and the conversation stops there, he is silenced by the idea, a philosopher, what does this mean. Are philosophers exempt from work, who supports them, what do they do exactly. He supposes that philosophers have no time for the ordinary errands of the world, and perhaps this is why Reiner is irritated by all his running around.

What would you prefer to be doing.

Walking.

We do walk.

Not enough. We should be in training for this trip. We must get into a routine, I can see you aren't fit.

Once Reiner makes them go on a long hike. We need a challenge, he says. To prepare us. They take a bus to Kloofnek, they walk along the pipe track past Camps Bay and almost to Llandudno, the landscape here with its grey stone and turquoise sea is very like Greece, the past echoes in concentric rings through time, they climb up over the top of the mountain and down the other side at Constantia Nek and from there through forest all the way back to Rondebosch, six or seven hours have gone by, their feet are blistered, they are dizzy with hunger. I feel faint, he says, I must eat. I also feel faint, Reiner says, it is an interesting feeling, I don't want to eat.

This is another difference between them, what is painful to the one is interesting to the other. The South African also loves to walk, but not constantly and obsessively, he is also drawn to extremity, but not when it becomes dangerous and threatening, he is incapable of examining his own pain like a spore on a slide and finding it interesting, interesting. If your own pain is interesting to you, how much more detached will you be from somebody else's pain, and it's true that there is something in Reiner that looks at all human failings with dispassion, maybe even with disdain. What has given rise to this coldness in him I don't know.

What Reiner wants is to be preparing with single-mindedness for this trip, he would like to dispense with all external trivia, the words he used on the balcony that night express some basic truth for him, people need too many things it is not necessary. He sits studying that map of Lesotho for hours, he has traced out in it a series of possible routes in red pen. I look at these thin lines with fear, they are like veins going through some strange internal organ, it feels at times that for Reiner this country is only a concept, some abstract idea that can be subjugated to the will. When he talks it's in terms of distances and altitudes, spatial dimensions that can be collapsed into formulas, there is no mention of people or history, nothing matters except himself and the empty place he's projecting himself into. What about the politics, I say, we haven't looked at the human situation, we don't know what we're getting into. Reiner stares at him with bemusement, then waves a contemptuous hand. Even here in South Africa, where he has never been, Reiner has no interest in what is happening around him, when he goes on his long walks through the streets he has a pair of earplugs that he pushes into his ears, he doesn't want external noises to intrude, his dark intense stare goes out ahead of him but is in reality turned inward.

But at this point there are only dim intimations of unease. He is excited about the trip. The little bit of friction between Reiner and himself will go, he is sure, when they are out of the city and alone together on the road. Neither of them was made for sedentary living.

He borrows a tent from a friend. Reiner insists that they put it up in the garden outside the flat. It takes a long time, the poles and pegs are like a strange new alphabet they have to learn. Everything must be borrowed or bought, gas-stove and cylinders water-filter torch knives and forks plastic plates a basic medicine-kit, he has never travelled in this way before, the strangeness of everything scares him, but it thrills him too, the thought of casting away his normal life is like freedom, the way it was when they met each other in Greece. And maybe that is the true reason for this journey, by shedding all the ballast of familiar life they are each trying to recapture a sensation of weightlessness they remember but perhaps never lived, in memory more than anywhere else travelling is like free-fall, or flight.

At some time in those last two weeks the question of money comes up. There are practical questions to be considered, such as how they will pay for themselves along the way. Reiner says that he has Canadian dollars that he wants to use up and so it's best if he is in charge of money. But what about me, I say.

You can pay me back later.

So I should write down what I spend.

Reiner nods and shrugs, money is trivial, it is not important.

Now everything is prepared. He finds himself saying good-bye to people with an edge of uneasiness, as if he might not be coming back. In every departure, deep down and tiny, like a black seed, there is the fear of death.

T hey take a train into the city. At the station they get onto a bus and ride through the night. It's difficult to sleep and they keep jolting awake to see the metallic grey landscape sliding past outside. They arrive in Bloemfontein at first light on a Sunday and walk through the deserted streets till they find a taxi rank from where they can get a minibus taxi to the Lesotho border. They have to wait for hours until the taxi is full. Reiner sits on the back seat, his rucksack on his knees and his head on his rucksack, earplugs wedged into his ears.

I wander around and come back, then wander again. A large part of travelling consists purely in waiting, with all the attendant ennui and depression. Memories come back of other places he has waited in, departure halls of airports, bus stations, lonely kerbsides in the heat, and in all of them there is an identical strain of melancholy summed up in a few transitory details. A paper bag blowing in the wind. The mark of a dirty shoe on a tile. The irregular sputter of a fluorescent bulb. From this particular place he will retain the vision of a cracked brick wall growing hotter and hotter in the sun.

When they leave it is already afternoon. The drive isn't far, a little over an hour, and they pass through a flat country of farmland, dirt roads going off on either side. They are the focus of unspoken curiosity in the crowded vehicle. Reiner is palpably unhappy at this enforced proximity to people, he has the air of someone holding his breath.

At the other end they get out into queues waiting to go through customs, the uniforms and dark glasses and barricades and discoloured rooms the elements of all border crossings. They pass through and over a long bridge across a river and are stamped through again on the other side. Now they have crossed a line on a map and are inside another country, in which the potentialities of fate are different from the ones they've left behind.

Where they go and what they do from here is unknown, he had some idea that they would simply set out, the road unrolling before them, but what they are confronted with instead is a sprawling border city, hotels and casinos on both sides of a dirty thoroughfare, crowds milling idly on the pavements, and it is already late in the day. They consult and decide that they will take a room for the night. Tomorrow they will abandon rooms for good. One hotel is as bad as another, they settle for the first one on the left, they are given a room high up over the street.

To pass the time they go walking around this city, Maseru. They go up and down the main street, they look at shops, they go to a supermarket and buy some food. Between them there is an excitement made partly from fear, they are committed to a situation of which the outcome is unknown, travel and love have this much in common. He doesn't love Reiner but their companionship does have the shape of a dark passion in it.

When they get back to the hotel they walk around there too. They go down the back steps into the garden. There is a wooden shed in the corner. A sign on the door says sauna. Inside is a woman of about fifty, something in her eyes is worn-out and finished, she is feverishly pleased to see them. Come in, come in, have a sauna. The sauna is tepid with no steam, the walls are just the wooden walls of the shed. No, no, we were just looking, maybe later. No, come now, have a massage, I give you a good massage. She is actually holding onto our arms.

When we get outside he says to Reiner, she was selling herself.

Reiner says nothing, but something in his expression is an answer nevertheless. He is silent and brooding all the way through supper in the dining room and upstairs again in the room. It's still early, but the rest of the evening stretches pointlessly away.

I think I will go out, Reiner says.

Where to.

Maybe I will have a sauna.

He goes out and I stand at the window for a long time, thinking. The lights of the city spread in every direction, but a deep darkness rings them round. He waits for Reiner to come back, but he doesn't come and doesn't come, and eventually he goes to bed.

When he wakes again it's morning and Reiner is on the other bed with only the cover over him. The cloth has fallen down and he isn't wearing anything underneath. The German is always delicate and fastidious about covering his body, and this careless abandonment feels like an announcement of some kind. The long brown back narrows down to the place where the buttocks divide, where paler skin makes fur and shadow stand out in relief, now Reiner turns, there is the briefest flash of an erection before his sleeping hand pulls up the cover, I get up in a turmoil of longing and revulsion, did he really do that last night.

Yes, he says.

You went back and slept with that woman.

Yes. He is smiling again, a thin supercilious smile, this is later in the day, he is sitting on the edge of the bed with a towel around his waist. Some part of Reiner is perpetually balanced on a high rocky crag, looking down on the moral confusion of the plain. When I was in Canada I started sleeping with whores.

Why.

I have a lot of tension. Sex helps me to get rid of tension.

This isn't an answer to the question but he doesn't ask again, it's obvious that he is perturbed and somehow this has made him weak, he nods and changes the subject but in his mind he cannot let go of the lined exhausted face of the woman in the sauna, the way she held onto our arms.

They dress and pack up and go. Only now are they truly departing, all the rest has been preparation. With the rucksacks on their backs they walk, the height and nature of the surrounding buildings change, but the city continues and continues. They are heading towards a high ridge at the eastern edge, hours go by but they seem to get no closer, it begins to appear that they will spend their second night here too.

But then they are on the long dirt road that climbs the ridge and slowly the tin roofs and gardens drop away till they are ascending the final slope with brown rocks and scrub on either side. When they reach the top they pause for one last look back into the simmering miasmic pot from which they've climbed and then go on. There is another ridge behind the first and now they are in a different place.

Mountains go on and on, the world of right angles and rigid lines has been subsumed into one of undulations and dips, graphs that chart moods in striations of colour, browns deepening into shades of blue that almost blur into the sky. It is late afternoon. But hot. Objects at the roadside, a tree, a broken plough, wax and wane in the fuming air. At first the landscape is empty, untilled and unworked, but over the next rise, or perhaps the next, there are fields, maybe tiny human figures toiling, a hut or a house in the distance. They stop and rest in a shady spot, it is incredible to him, perhaps to both of them, that they are here, what was an unconsidered line in a letter months ago has come to pass.

They walk and walk, all the motion latent in the vast curves of the earth somehow contracted into the dynamics of this movement, one leg swinging past the other, each foot planted and uprooted in turn, the whole surface of the world has been trodden down just like this over time. The rucksack is heavy, the belt cuts into his hips and shoulders, his toes and heels are chafing in his boots, his mouth is dry, all the loose and disconnected thoughts of his brain cohere around the will and impulse to go on. Alone he would not. Alone he would sit down and not move again, or alone he would not be here at all, but he is here and this fact in itself makes him subservient to the other, who pulls him along in his wake as if on thin threads of power.

They do not talk. There is, yes, an occasional conversation, but about practical things, where will we sleep, should we have a rest, otherwise they walk, sometimes next to each other, sometimes apart, but always alone. It's strange that all this space, unconfined by artificial limits as it spills to the horizon, should throw you back so completely into yourself, but it does, I don't know when I was last so intensely concentrated into a single point, see me walking on that dust road with my face washed clean of all the usual emotions, the strains and strivings to link up with the world. Maybe deep meditation makes you feel that way. And maybe that is what Reiner means when he says that night that walking has a rhythm that takes you over.

What do you mean.

If you walk and walk for long enough, the rhythm takes over.

There is a vagueness to the way he says this that makes you want to leave the topic there, this is often the case with Reiner, he offers a thought that's interesting or profound and perhaps not his own, and on the other side of it you sense a blankness that he can't fill up, there are no further thoughts to follow on. He waits in silence for you to speak. Sometimes you do, but not tonight, I am too tired, they are sitting side by side in a small cave, an overhang in the rock.

It is almost dark. This is hours and hours after they left the city, he would have liked to stop long ago but Reiner wanted to continue, only after the sun has set does he finally concede that it's time to pitch the tent, but now there is nowhere that looks hospitable, there are fields on one side and a bare ridge on the other, this is too exposed, it feels wrong, let's just go over the ridge and take a look. And there by chance they find the cave, Reiner has the calm triumphant look of someone who knew all the time, what his look implies is that he is attuned to the rhythms of the universe, the rhythms of walking no different to those of living, go bravely to extremes and everything will be provided. See, no need to put up the tent. I am less enthusiastic, are we really going to do this, sleep out in the open like a pair of tramps, he is spoiled and soft, he lacks the fatalism of his hard companion, and shepherds have shat in little piles around the cave. But as it gets darker and the world contracts to the size of the tiny overhang, it is more pleasant to be here, in the circle of firelight they've made with their hands.

In front of the cave the earth drops away into a vast valley, in the light the hugeness of this space was frightening but now it has become consoling, far far below are the tiny isolated fires of herdsmen, the distant sound of cowbells carries up in quavering echoes, when they have boiled water and eaten a sense of well-being descends, all the rifts and ruptures of the world knitted up and healed, hours of sleep ahead.

He spreads his sleeping bag and lies down on one side, staring out into the dark. After a moment Reiner comes over and crouches down behind him. They say nothing, the silence thickens into tension and then Reiner says, in one of your letters.

Yes.

You said you were looking forward to seeing me again.

Yes.

What did you mean by that.

He doesn't know what he meant by that but he knows what Reiner means by this. He can't help it, but all day on the road his mind has conjured images it doesn't want, he keeps seeing that woman from last night, filled to the brim with such febrile desperation, he sees Reiner on top of her, bending her into plastic poses with his brown hands. What Reiner wants now would be no different than with the woman, a ritual performed without tenderness or warmth or sensual pleasure.

But the truth is also that there is an answering impulse of subservience in him, part of him wants to give in, I see shadows thrown up in grappling contortions on the roof of the cave.

I don't know what I meant.

You don't know what you meant.

I was looking forward to seeing you.

Nothing else.

Not that I can think of.

Reiner nods slowly. Neither of them is quite the person that by mutual agreement they have been till now, the rules will be different from tonight. He can smell the smoky sweat of the other man, or perhaps it is his own, not a bad smell, and then Reiner gets up and moves away to the far side of the cave to settle himself. They don't speak again. The fire slowly subsides, the shadows fade, the sound of bells continues in the air.

They leave again before it's light, the road still blue and indistinct. The sore places from yesterday ache with fresh intensity, but after half an hour of walking the pain has become dispersed and general. He hurts pleasantly all over. The sun comes up and on every side the mountains rise up out of the dark.

They are walking in a big circle that will end in a place close to the city again, from where they will begin a second and larger circle ending in almost the same place, from where they will begin a third. In this way they will traverse the country in three growing loops, the last of which will take them into the highest mountains of the Drakensberg, far off in the east. By then they hope to be fit and strong, more used to the hardships of this kind of travel, though he has his doubts. It is Reiner who has planned their journey this way, marking it out in coloured ink on his map.

They stop at a little roadside shop to buy food for the day. The tiny room is full of tins and boxes and packets, pasta and sweets and vegetables and soap. The packs are heavy and it seems sensible to get light things, some rolls maybe, some rice. But Reiner stalks around the dim interior of the shop, selecting heavy items from the shelves, he chooses tins, a bag of potatoes, bars of chocolate.

But why.

I feel like it.

Chocolate.

I like chocolate. I read an article about a man who lived for a year on chocolate and water.

It isn't possible.

Reiner looks at him, smirking, of course it's possible. In the days to come he will break off little pieces of chocolate and eat delicately, savouring some essence in it that will nourish him beyond the laws of biology. For Reiner the complexities and contradictions of the world are a distraction, and the truth is always stark and simple, a rule that must be followed rigidly if all the confusion is to be overcome, it is possible, he believes, to survive on will-power and chocolate, and every time he offers any to his companion that little smirk returns to Reiner's face.

The money that pays for this food, as well as for everything else, is Reiner's. In Maseru he changed some of his Canadian dollars into rands, he carries the money in a pouch around his waist, and this is what they're living on now. Although I note down each item diligently in a little notebook, and will repay every cent at the end of the trip, what becomes clear even now, on the second day of this journey, is that Reiner will decide what they may or may not have along the way.

So they take the tins and potatoes and chocolate, they distribute them evenly, but their weight feels disproportionately heavy when they set out again, he feels pulled down by a strong resentment, he walks more slowly than before. By noon the sun is intensely hot, both of them are pouring sweat. They are near some ugly modern buildings, a little village of some kind, there is an old ruined church. I think we should stop and rest for a bit, Reiner says.

Over the top of the ridge on the right there is a steep drop, halfway down is a cave larger than the one they slept in last night, Reiner wants to climb to it. But it's a long way down. So what. So we have to climb back up again. So what. There is another moment of unspoken conflict, the sardonic mockery in the dark eyes of the one man wins over the reluctance of the weaker man, they pick their way down between boulders and aloes, loose pebbles scattering under their feet. When they come to the cave his anger cools in the shade of the stone, the calm vista of the valley that unrolls at their feet. It's beautiful here. Yes. What he means by that one syllable of agreement is that he is right again.

They throw themselves down on the rock. He falls asleep and when he wakes hours have gone by and it is starting to storm. The sky is black and blue with cloud, ladders of lightning drop down, thunder shakes the stone. When the rain comes it is almost solid, a door closing off the world. They sit under the ceiling of rock, water pouring down, with cool scents leaking up out of the ground. It is like last night, now that he is rested and refreshed, now that the heat has gone, the rawness of his extreme emotions is also soothed, he can almost love this strange place he finds himself in, and his strange companion too.

I think, Reiner says, we should travel every day like this. We should get up early and walk and then stop in the middle of the day. Then we go again.

Yes, he says.

At this moment he is in full agreement with Reiner, he doesn't know how he could have been angry with him, against the stormy sky his solemn face is beautiful.

When the storm clears the light comes through and they go out into a world rinsed clean and dripping with colour. These afternoon storms happen almost every day, the heat will build in intensity till it finally breaks, afterwards there is always this feeling of regeneration, in the landscape but also between themselves.

They are truly on the road now. Until they spent their first night in the open this whole trip was still a mad idea, one they could abandon at any time, but somehow they have passed a point and gone from one world into another. In the old world they had their usual life, with its habits and friends, its places and choices, but now all that has been left behind. In this new life they have only each other and the selection of objects that they carry on their backs. Everything else, even the people they stop and speak to at the roadside, is passing by.

In this curious union, this bizarre marriage, a new set of habits must spring up to keep them alive. There are tasks that must be seen to, the most basic, the most necessary, that on certain days can be luminous with almost religious significance, and on others can feel like the most tedious of chores. The tent, for example, must be put up and taken down. Two or three times a day a meal must be prepared, then the pots and pans must afterwards be cleaned. In the beginning, for the first few days, these jobs are shared equally between them. They help each other lay out the poles and insert them through the limp canvas, cast around together for stones to knock the pegs into the ground. Or they trade, why don't you put up the tent, I'll make the supper. Okay, I'll help you wash up later. And although they are wary of each other, and the little moments of conflict do recur, there is a symmetry and balance to the running of things, they could continue like this for some time.

In these early days there is a lot of talking between them still, they find their way into interesting conversations, they exchange ideas and disagree with respect. And if they avoid personal topics, if there is no discussion of their most intimate lives, it is because they have left those intimate lives behind. In their place is this new intimacy, the practical one between them, in which they lie next to each other and bump against each other in the dark, and look into each other's faces first thing in the morning, and in a certain sense it's this intimacy that is the engine of their journey.

The day becomes organized around little rituals of collapse and renewal. Every morning they get up very early before it's light.

One of them makes a fire to boil water for coffee while the other takes down the tent. Then they set out, trying to cover a certain distance before it gets too hot. After an hour or two they stop to have breakfast. Then they wash up, if there is water, or store the dirty pots and plates till later, and set out again.

By the middle of the morning, when it becomes too hot, they find a place to rest for a few hours. In this country of peaks and valleys, threaded with rivers, there is often a shady spot near water, with a view out into blue distances, they become used to sleeping in these soft and lush surroundings, bees drone, the shadows of clouds move silently, grass waves.

Now the heat is building towards a storm. The edges of mountains take on a sharp electric sheen, in the high air thunderheads mount up, eventually a hot dry wind begins to blow. Either they will wait where they are, sometimes even putting up the tent again until the storm has come and gone, or they will take shelter in a hut or cave. Their greatest fear at these times is lightning. In this dislocated state, in which death is a constant presence beneath the skin, it is a grotesquely plausible idea that they will be struck down from the sky. He has never seen such brilliant fire, or heard such terrifying thunder.

Then there is the last walk of the day, the final push of energy and effort, trying to cover a particular distance before the night comes down. Around sunset they find a place to sleep. Most of the time they pitch the tent. If they are near a village they go to ask permission from the chief, this is invariably granted, once or twice they are offered a room to sleep in. Then there are the evening rituals, the fire and food, perhaps a little reading, the walk out into the dark with a toilet-roll in hand. Before it is very late they sleep, stretching out side by side, exhaustion erases the mind in seconds, even the hardest ground is soft.

So the days go on. The road takes them past houses, or little clusters of huts, and everywhere people stop what they're doing to watch them go past. Sometimes greetings are shouted, stock English phrases they must have learned at school, hello how are you yes no I am also fine goodbye. In many places crowds of children swarm around them, following with singing and laughter this pair of pied pipers who draw them in their wake. In one village the mayor puts them up in his house, he is a huge gap-toothed man who smokes marijuana incessantly in rolls of newspaper, he insists on giving them his own bed to sleep in while he spends the night somewhere else. At a roadside store two schoolgirls chat shyly, they also try out their litany of English phrases, hello hello what is your name, then one blurts out I love you and both of them collapse in giggles.

Reiner finds the schoolgirls amusing, I could have a fat wife in Lesotho, I would like that ho ho ho, but to most of these friendly overtures he responds with irritation. He doesn't want to be bothered with smiling and talking, he sees no need for interaction of this kind. He puts in his earplugs when he sets out in the morning, he keeps his eyes fixed ahead of him on the road. He is happy to be offered a room, but he doesn't want to pay for it, and he doesn't want to ask permission to camp. Why should we. It's the custom. Their custom, not mine. This is their country we're in. Their country, I don't believe in countries, that's just lines on a map. Sometimes I don't know what you do believe in, Reiner. To this the sulky face only smiles.

Most of the time they follow the road, but sometimes they go across country. This happens when Reiner sees a place on his map where they can cut across, look here, from this point to there. But there are mountains in between. Yes, I see them.

Often it seems he chooses these routes precisely because of the obstacles, mountains, rivers, escarpments, they present an interesting challenge, we must overcome nature with the same dispassion it shows us, so they walk out into the wilderness.

I don't like leaving the road, my sense of vulnerability deepens, a sort of primal nervousness descends. But this is also one of the most compelling elements in travel, the feeling of dread underneath everything, it makes sensations heightened and acute, the world is charged with a power it doesn't have in ordinary life.

After about a week they complete the first loop of their journey. In the little town of Roma they camp in the grounds of a deserted seminary, the long sandstone building with its pillars and arches, a dark row of poplar trees behind it, like something out of Italy.

In Roma too there is the very old man in the pavement restaurant at lunchtime, where are you from, smiling toothlessly all the time, ah South Africa you people think we are monkeys you keep Nelson Mandela in prison. When he tells him that Nelson Mandela is out of jail, three years ago already, the old man laughs uproariously, throwing his head back, you think we are monkeys, Nelson Mandela is locked up. But he isn't, he isn't, I promise you, somehow he almost wants to cry. The old man laughs at him, hating him, leave it, Reiner says, looking panicked, he doesn't know, nobody's told him, leave it.

The next day they walk out of Roma and follow roads that take them into high mountains. Till then they have been in the foothills of the Drakensberg, now the peaks climb around them in weird fantastic lines against the sky. The road rises and falls like a boat on rough seas, it pinches into hairpin bends and goes into elaborate loops to cover short distances. In the afternoon there is a bad storm. The sky above the long valley closes over, the lightning is spectacular. They shelter outside a house and afterwards push on, looking for a flat place to pitch the tent, but there is none, the road is halfway up the side of the valley with steep walls above and below. As darkness falls they come to a mission station, it turns out that the priests are German, Reiner has a long and amiable conversation, smiling and nodding, he is like another person completely. The priests say they have no space but send them to the chief of the local village, they sleep that night on the mud floor of a hut, mysterious rustlings from the thatch overhead.

Reiner says that the priests have told him the road they are on comes to an end not far ahead. From there they will have to walk across rough country to the next road. Reiner has a plan, look, he says, we can do it, he wants to try a long hike next day, the longest they've done so far, all the way to Semonkong.

By now even the most trivial events conceal some kind of groping for power. In the very beginning, two years ago, when they first saw each other in Greece, they thought of themselves as the same. On that lonely road they looked like mirror images of each other. Perhaps each of them thought of real communication as unnecessary, words divide by multiplying, what was certain was the oneness underneath the words. But now they refrain from talking because it might reveal to them how dangerously unlike one another they are. An image in a mirror is a reversal, the reflection and the original are joined but might cancel each other out.

So underneath the journey is a conflict, almost another journey in itself, a struggle for ascendancy, which as the days go by begins to push through to the surface. When they get up in the morning Reiner has taken to bathing himself, either in a river, if there is one, or in water from the water-bottles. Then he dries himself and sits on a rock, rubbing creams and lotions into his skin, which he dispenses from a selection of little jars and vials. Then he takes out a wooden hairbrush and runs it through his long hair, stroke after stroke, till it shines. Although this ritual gets longer every day, until it takes up half an hour or more, Reiner is always careful to be willing to do his share, just wait a little while and I will help you, leave the tent I'll do it, but his companion can't bear watching, it is better to keep busy, to make coffee, to put away the tent, while Reiner preens. When they set out a little later he is often choked with anger or irritation, and Reiner is full of smug satisfaction, brown locks bouncing on his shoulders.

A second point of conflict is money. He has been keeping meticulous records in his little book, to which Reiner is apparently indifferent. But whenever they stop to buy something there is a silent battle about what they will choose and who will be allowed to have it. Reiner continues to buy his chocolates, for example, but if I want something there is often a dispute, hmm I don't know about that what do we need that for. And sometimes Reiner will buy something for himself, a box of sweets or a bottle of water, and wait for his companion to ask. The asking is humiliating, which Reiner knows. Money is never just money alone, it is a symbol for other deeper things, on this trip how much you have is a sign of how loved you are, Reiner hoards the love, he dispenses it as a favour, I am endlessly gnawed by the absence of love, to be loveless is to be without power.

So at this point of the journey there are the moments of unity and the other moments of conflict, and the long separate spaces of walking in between, in which each of them is alone. But even in this activity they cannot agree. It is not enough that they should go from A to B, but they have to do it in a certain time, it's not enough that they should follow the road, they must always be going up to that rock or down to that cave, something is always being measured, something is always being pushed. At night Reiner is forever crouched over his map with a torch, adding up the kilometres they've covered, checking the distance against the time.

So when he says he wants to do the long hike tomorrow, it means something different to both of them.

How far is it.

About sixty kilometres.

In one day.

We can do it.

But why.

Because I want to get better.

He understands that Reiner is pitting himself against certain odds, the limitations of himself, the adversity of conditions, in this scheme of things he is one more resistance to be overcome, he doesn't like to be seen this way and so he says, yes, well, we can try.

They get up long before sunrise. By the time it starts to become light they have long since quit the mud house of the chief and are on the road. For much of yesterday they were above the forested floor of the valley, but now as the mountains draw in on either side the road drops down, till they come to a village. The road ends here. They sit for a while among the houses and rough gardens, goats grazing amiably in the flowers, chickens pecking in the dirt. Then they set off, striking out in a general direction, this must be the way. They have to climb out of the valley, over the mountains, the route goes up and up. These are the steepest slopes they've had to deal with, no road could ascend like this, they are scrabbling for a foothold much of the time, there are paths occasionally, which they follow, the paths take them to villages, yes even here in the precipitous wastes there are the congregations of round huts with the area of packed dry soil between them, the faces peering out in curiosity or amazement as they go by, people living out their whole lives in one small portion of the earth, oblivious to anything beyond. Memory is patchy and intermittent again, why are certain vistas, certain stretches of a path, so deeply impressed in recollection, so vividly evoked, and others disappear without a trace, I see the two of them at last climbing up a final slope to the bare crown of a hill, there are other villages on top, fields of maize, but off in the distance higher up there is the line of the road, a car perhaps passing like a toy on a track, we made it, look look, we're here.

It takes another hour to reach the road. A deep fatigue has already settled in, they sit outside a house to rest. Cars pass from time to time, they could hitch a ride, but this would defeat the purpose, in a little while they go on. The sky today is flawless, a huge heat presses down. They come to a shop on the shoulder of a hill, now there is no longer the will or energy to continue, they sit on the concrete stoep outside, he passes out for a while, and they are only halfway there.

When they go on it's along a rural country track that lifts out of this populous plateau, then they are on a high deserted heath with distances devoid of people, nothing moves except themselves, and then barely. They are very tired by now. The relentless uphill since the morning has depleted them, although they are gently descending now their muscles are strained to breaking point, there is no pleasure in this movement at all. Not even Reiner is happy. There are no signposts or settlements, the map can't tell them where they are, I keep my eyes ahead, looking for Semonkong, we must almost be there, surely by now we must be there, but around every bend the road continues, unrolling ahead of them like fate. A man on a donkey in an enormous Basuto hat and blanket goes past, he pays them no mind. The road drops down more steeply, they are lowering again from the highest point in this range, the sun slides down behind the peaks.

On the other side of exhaustion there is a state of weakness so acute that it ceases to matter where you are or what you are doing. This state comes down over him in the evening, he feels a lassitude like sleep, it is difficult to balance. He passes a horse in a field under a full moon. No other image from this journey is so rare and brilliant for him, the green of the grass like glossy plumage, the animal dreaming quietly in profile, the white circle up above like God. Surely now they must be there. But full night comes down, not a light anywhere, they go on.

This is enough, he says to Reiner. Why don't we stop.

Here. Reiner looks around, even his drawn and fractured face is tempted, but he won't give in. We must be so close, we've come so far already.

At the base of the mountains the road flattens out, surely now, surely now, they walk without stopping because if they rested they would not get up, they pass a dam, birds fly up shrieking at their passage, the wild cries in the night are like the voice of the ground calling stop now stop, but they don't stop, the landscape passing on either side is moving now of its own volition, it has nothing to do with their walking, far above the stars wheel imperceptibly in their cryptic patterns, the perfect circle of the moon rolls like a lost hoop and disappears, sometime towards midnight they come over a rise and ahead of them are the low flat shapes, the scattered sullen lights of the town. A dog begins to bark, another takes it up, on a wave of snarls and yelps they are buoyed through the streets, who are these wanderers come in out of the dark.

There is a sign. They follow. Through the town and out the other side. The road drops down into a gorge and crosses a river, they come to a campsite at the bottom with bungalows spread out, all is in darkness. They ring a bell, someone comes, they are too tired to put up the tent so they take a room, they get into bed. We did it, Reiner says, we have succeeded, but he knows without thinking it that the thread has been stretched too far.

They rest there for a couple of days. In the morning they move out of the bungalow and pitch their tent on the grass. There is a belt of trees and then the river, flowing brown as beer between the rocks.

They hardly speak now. Both of them have been hit hard by the long hike, their feet are blistered, their muscles ache, there are raw patches that the rucksacks have worn down on their skin. But their responses to this experience are very different. Reiner seems rejuvenated, the point for him was to overcome his weakness and the point has been achieved, already he is planning the next stage of their journey. He announces that they can walk for perhaps a day on a good road, which goes up to a certain place. Between this place and the end of the second loop of the walk is a range of mountains with no road going through. If they alter their course, if they travel south a little way, they will come to a road that would take them directly to where they're trying to go, but this is too easy, let's walk across, Reiner says. Two days, three days, we'll be there.

I stare dully at the map.

I would like to do more long hikes, Reiner says. Like this last one. What do you think. We build up, then we do a big walk, then we rest for a few days.

He nods, he turns away, something inside him is finished. The tiredness of the long walk will not leave his body, a numbness has crept into his bones. He wanders around the campsite, trying to revive, he thinks about everything and resolves nothing, he washes his clothes in the river and drapes them over the rocks to dry. Then he sits in the sun, listening to the water, reading. In a strange room you must empty yourself for sleep. And before you are emptied for sleep, what are you. And when you are emptied for sleep, you are not. And when you are filled with sleep, you never were. The words come to him from a long way off. He puts the book down and stares at peculiar long-legged insects on the surface of the river, they dart frantically back and forth, living out their whole lives in a space of one or two metres, they know nothing about him or his troubles, even now they're unaware of him watching, their otherness to him is complete.

The owner of the campsite is a fat man called John. He tells them about a spectacular view an hour and a half's walk away, don't miss it, he says, it's really something. When they get there it turns out to be true, the view is truly astonishing, the same river they're camped beside falls over a cliff and disappears into space. He lies down on his stomach and peers over the edge. The drop goes on and on, dizzying, vertiginous, in it gravity is compounded with a secret longing for death.

When he crawls away and stands he sees Reiner a little way off, on a boulder at the edge of the cliff, leaning against the abyss. What passes across his mind then, fleetingly, wordless, is the urge to push, one tiny movement of my hands and he is gone. Where does it come from, this thought of murder surfacing so casually amongst the everyday debris of my brain and then sinking away again.

This is the way we have to walk, Reiner says. Tomorrow.

Oh.

When we go on, I would like to do a night-hike. We leave when it gets dark, we go on all night.

We can try that, he says.

So the next afternoon they set off together in the last light as a fine rain starts to fall. They disappear into darkness, and into a hole in memory too, the next picture I have is of the two of them, in stark daylight again, climbing through the mountains. They have left the road and are heading roughly west. On this hot ordinary day, the two tiny figures wend their way up, up, between crevasses and fissures and fields and koppies, passing villages and little streams, dense copses and woods of trees, heading towards the top of the range, from where they will be able to begin their descent. Reiner is driving them on. It rains in the afternoon, a brief intense downpour, but the heat doesn't go away. Steam rises on every side, as if the earth is smouldering, and in the late afternoon the air is taut and electric and hot.

Then everything seems to happen very quickly, converging towards a point. They come out on what feels like the roof of the world just as dusk is falling, with a precipitous gorge directly in front of them and line upon line of mountains rippling away. The dark is coming down unnaturally fast and when they look out ahead of them they see why. Rolling in from separate points on the horizon are two massive storms, their paths set to collide roughly where they are standing. The black fronts of cloud are impenetrable, already the sun is obscured.

It's too late now to retrace their steps, or to find a place lower down to shelter. There are only a few minutes left before the storms will hit, just enough time to put up the tent, and they start fumbling frantically with poles and pegs and straps. The wind is rising and there is a strange smell, like metal, on the air. The sound of thunder comes again and again. They get the tent up and the rucksacks inside and then they rush around finding rocks to weigh down the canvas.

By now the outlines of the world are bending and wavering, and it feels as if they're rushing through space. With a calm eye somewhere in his brain he observes how very exposed and isolated they are, this one little bump standing up on the bald crown of the mountain.

The lightning, he thinks, we must get rid of the metal. For the next minute or two they rummage through the bags, collecting all the metal they can find. Laden with cutlery and pen-knives and bracelets they rush out again and throw the little pitiful heap of silver down in the roiling undergrowth and rush back. Would it make any difference, this ridiculous precaution, there are still the pegs in the ground, also metal, too late to do anything about those. They climb back inside as the storms strike.

No human force has prepared him for a violence so imper-sonal or strong. Wind and rain and noise. The ground shakes. Between the lightning and the thunder the interval is tiny and getting smaller. Then there is no interval and the centre of power is above them.

Somehow this image sums it up, this is the moment it has all led to, he lies face down towards the back of the tent, like a piece of wood, a stone, his head pressed into the ground and his hands over his ears. Now, he thinks, it will happen now, now, now, while Reiner lies the other way, his head up, holding the flaps of the entrance slightly apart so that he can look out, with that sulky expression of an angry child, at the roaring world lit up like noon.

The morning dawns perfect and cloudless. He wakes early and crawls out into calm. The bushes are silver with moisture, the mountains are crisp and clear against the blue. In the clean air the eye travels with telescopic power to the tiny details of the horizon. They are very high up.

Reiner emerges a while later and looks around. Hmm, he says. I think I will take a little walk. He wanders off in the direction of the gorge.

While he waits for Reiner he lights the stove to make some tea and then inspects the damage of last night. Some of the ropes have come loose, and some of the rocks have rolled, but otherwise the tent is secure. More than anything, their weight must have held it down.

Reiner is still not back, so he busies himself by dragging the rucksacks out of the tent. Then he starts to pack it all up. This takes more time than usual because of all the mud and dirt, and when the plastic has been rolled up and stowed he can't find some of the pegs. They've sunk into the wet ground and disappeared.

Reiner reappears, striding in through the undergrowth. His silence says that he is truly in his element here, on the steeple of the world, among storms and peaks.

I can't find all the pegs.

Hmm, Reiner says. He helps himself to tea and goes to sit on a rock, staring out intensely into the distance.

He digs in the mud for a bit, then wanders off to look for the metal they threw away last night. He can't remember where they put it, nothing looks today the way it did in the dark. Eventually the glint of silver catches his eye and he carries it back in a bristling pile to put away. Reiner watches him and says, you were scared of the lightning.

Yes. Weren't you.

He shakes his head and sips his tea.

I make breakfast. Reiner throws out the last of his tea and comes over to eat. They don't talk and there is a deep tension, some remnant of the electric thrill of the storm, between them. Reiner eats slowly, thinking and staring, and he's still busy when his companion finishes. He is impatient with waiting and goes off again to look for the missing pegs. When he next looks Reiner is perched on a rock, his shirt off, rubbing cream into his skin.

Don't you want to help me look.

I'm busy, Reiner says.

Busy.

He comes back and collects the dirty plates and cutlery together. He stows them in his bag and by then Reiner has finished rubbing and has started brushing his hair. The brush flickers, the strokes go on, repetitive and infuriating.

He goes off to clean his teeth. When he gets back Reiner has finished brushing and is putting his shirt on. Then he also squeezes out toothpaste onto his toothbrush and wanders off.

He comes back a few minutes later at a quick, efficient pace. Ready, he says, let's go.

We haven't found all the pegs yet.

What.

The pegs.

Reiner clicks his tongue in irritation, he sighs. He comes over to the flattened patch where the tent was pitched and peers around at the trampled ground. After a few moments he says, leave them.

What.

Leave them. We'll use something else.

It's not my tent. I have to take care of it.

Well, they're gone. I can't see them. Come on, we've wasted a lot of time this morning.

He looks at him and from a long way inside words travel up through great resistance, he says, you haven't done anything.

What.

You haven't done anything. I've done everything this morning. I want to look for the pegs.

Reiner gives again that impatient click, he tosses his long hair expressively. Without a word he picks up his rucksack and sets off along the footpath they've been following. The one left behind stares in amazement as he strides off, his dark figure shrinking rapidly till it disappears. Then he puts the tent away in his bag and starts to follow.

The path goes at first through lots of twists and turns, following the contour of the hill, he can't see far ahead, but as he comes around the side of the mountain the slope opens out and the path unravels a long way into the future. Now he can see Reiner in the distance, a tiny figure, moving fast and not looking back. He tries to speed up, but he is tired and heavy. He is also carrying more than his share, it is Reiner's job to carry the tent but he strode off without it, everything in the end is coming down to a few lost pegs and the weight of a tent.

After a while he stops trying to catch up. But when they are on the other side of the mountain he gets a full view of the path going on, then taking a sharp turn to the left and descending towards a river. Reiner is far along, approaching the turn. The path doesn't travel a direct route, and he sees that if he leaves the track here and cuts across a steep slope he can come out ahead of Reiner at the river.

He goes off down to the left, scrabbling between little scrubby bushes and loose rocks, trying to keep his balance. From the corner of his eye he watches Reiner, he sees him speed up when he realizes what's going on, trying to keep his lead, then slowing down again when he realizes he can't do it. All this happens without mutual acknowledgement.

Lurching and struggling, he comes to the bottom of the dip and rejoins the path ahead of Reiner. Now he can afford to relax. He takes a leisurely walk to the river and removes his pack and sits down to wait. The water is shallow but fast. Stones have been positioned so that you can hop from one to another to get across. Just over the crest of a rise on the far side are the pointed roofs of huts, a thin line of smoke cracking open the sky.

In a few minutes Reiner arrives. They don't look at each other. He stands, gazing around, then also takes his pack off and sits down. They don't speak. They both stare silently in the same direction, a little way apart from each other. The noise of water underscores the scene. Both of them are calm, and it is understood that they will proceed together from this point.

When they set off again it is Reiner who moves first, standing and stretching and busying himself with his pack. Then he also stands and prepares himself, mirroring Reiner. It's as if they're in different places, not a word has been spoken.

Halfway across, he slips on a stone and falls. He isn't hurt, only wet and humiliated. Reiner has already gone across safely and he turns to look back briefly. He doesn't laugh but it's as if he's laughing. He doesn't wait, he doesn't pause, he leaves me kneeling in the water and goes on, in half a minute he's disappeared over the rise.

I get up, walk across to the other side. Stare for a second at the empty path, thinking, he's gone again, he's gone again. Then follow. Powered now by a fury that makes him glacially calm, all the unsaid words swirling in his mouth like smoke, limbs hot with all the things he didn't do.

Over the rise he sees Reiner sitting in a dip, on a log, smiling as he watches children from the village playing in long grass around him. Smiling and smiling.

He comes up and says, why didn't you wait.

Reiner looks up, eyebrows raised, an expression of patient enquiry on his face.

When I fell just now. In the water. Why didn't you wait. I waited for you.

We will discuss it, Reiner says. But later.

We will discuss it now.

The last word, the now, is charged with a voltage that surprises everybody. The children, who haven't understood the meaning of this quiet exchange, suddenly go silent and move watchfully away.

We will discuss it, Reiner says, but not in that tone of voice.

His own tone is disdainful and bored, it's as if a bad smell has passed under his nose, he looks at his companion then back at the children and smiles.

What happens next I too am watching, I am a spectator of my own behaviour, opening the rucksack and taking things out and throwing them. Words are coming from my mouth too, also plucked out and thrown, incoherent and mismatched, their trajectories colliding, you think I enjoy walking with you I don't I don't enjoy it you can walk on your own from now on you're alone do you hear me how can you treat me here take this you'll need this and this and this, throwing the gas canisters, the bed-roll, knives and forks, toilet rolls, tins of food, and this and this and this.

The objects fly and hit the ground and bounce. Reiner watches them with an amused detachment, oh dear look at all this madness how unfortunate. He doesn't move. He appears to have been awaiting this moment from the outset, although the truth is probably that it's the last thing he expects.

Then the frenzy is finished, he closes his pack and picks it up, he starts to walk away. It is difficult to believe that he's doing this, part of him wants to be recalled, so when he hears Reiner's voice he stops.

Hey.

He turns. Reiner is walking towards him. If he offers one word of apology, if he concedes even the smallest humility, then I will relent. But Reiner is too rigid and too proud. Though what he does do is somehow even stranger.

Here, he says. You'll need this.

He is holding out a fifty rand note.

He has no money of his own, not a single cent, but in his fury was prepared to walk away penniless, and even now he hesitates. But then his hand comes out, he takes the money, this is a bitter farewell.

Goodbye.

Goodbye.

Or maybe there are no goodbyes, nothing spoken, yes it is more likely that way, the last glance passes between them and they turn their backs on each other. He starts to walk in a direction he hopes, judging by the sun and his instinct, is east. When he comes to the top of the ridge he looks back and Reiner has gathered all the objects and bits and pieces together and is going in the other direction, west. So they walk away from each other in the high mountains one morning, watched by the children in the grass.

I n half an hour he starts to feel regret. He acted passionately, he didn't think, it wasn't fair to abandon somebody like that. But immediately answering voices clamour, what else should you have done, he deserved to be abandoned. He stops and sits and thinks, holding his head in his hands. He tries to consider his options. But what point is there, even if he tries to catch up with Reiner there is no way of knowing where he is in these mountains, and if he does find him how likely is it that this fight can be resolved. He knows in his bones that Reiner does not forgive.

So he shoulders his pack and goes on, walking faster and more lightly now than he has in days. He continues to head east, trying to get back to Semonkong. Whenever he comes to a settlement of any kind, a shop or a village, he stops and asks, and there is invariably somebody who knows the way. At one place a serene young man in blue overalls insists on coming along to be his guide, walking for miles next to him, not talking, just smiling shyly whenever he is asked something. He leads him to the mouth of a ravine that cuts down through the mountains. There is a footpath descending and he points, this way Semonkong, smiling and bobbing his head.

There is no money to give him, only the fifty rand note, but the young man doesn't seem to expect payment, he accepts a handshake happily and watches the strange traveller depart. The walls of rock mount up on either side, the ravine seems empty of people, but a little way on a shepherd, invisible high up above somewhere, starts calling to him, the same phrases he's heard before, learned by rote at school, hello hello how are you. He looks but can see nothing. Hello I love you, the big voice shouts, echoing surreally down the gorge, I love you I love you hello.

Asking and wandering, he finds his way back to Semonkong by evening. This is an achievement, he's covered two days' journey in one, but maybe his route is more direct, and his pack is certainly lighter. The fat man John seems confused to see him again so soon, didn't you leave two days ago, and where is that other guy, the German. We had a fight in the mountains, we parted company. John allows him to camp for the night at half the usual cost, he is helpful but suspicious, maybe he murdered his companion in the hills. But in the morning he comes and suggests, you see that girl there, she's driving to Maseru today, maybe she'll give you a lift.

The girl is a woman of twenty four or five, an American working on some relief programme in Lesotho. She isn't happy to help, he can see from her expression, but she agrees, he will have to ride in the back with some of her co-workers and a pile of boxes she has to unload. Yes yes anything that will be fine. He climbs in with the others and listens to them bicker and squabble among themselves. They have been here too long with each other, he can hear a certain note in their voices, it is time for them to go home.

Today he himself is feeling stunned and empty, he can't quite credit the rapid end to events, he keeps playing that scene of yesterday in his mind. He closes his ears to the conversation around him and looks out through the window at the countryside passing by. It's strange to be seeing in reverse the whole extended panorama of the long walk they did just days ago, here is the spot where we rested, there's the place where I saw the horse, that's where we joined up with the road.

They come to Roma in the late morning. This is where the boxes have to be unloaded, he goes with the others to the compound where they're housed, he helps them carry the boxes and waits in the shade for them to finish their other business. He can tell that they find him odd and aloof, his silence is an eccentricity to them, but he can't engage in all the right social cues, he is alone.

It's hours before they get going again, and then another hour or so to Maseru. She drops him at the outer edge of the city, she is heading off somewhere else and can't be bothered to run him further, but he is effusive in his thanks. Goodbye, goodbye. Then with his rucksack on his back he goes walking the length of the endless main street again.

By the time he gets through the two border crossings it is late afternoon. Now suddenly he is thrown back on the physical realities of his situation, which are not comforting or good. At some point in the last day he has decided to go back north, up to Pretoria where his mother lives, because it's closer and easier than Cape Town. But now that he is finally stranded at the roadside with the red sun going down ahead of him it makes no difference what his destination is. He has used up twenty rand on campsite and food, he has thirty rand with which to travel six hundred kilometres. And this is not the benevolent deserted landscape of Lesotho, this is a border crossing in South Africa, cars and vans continually pass him by, streams of people go up and down the road, he is a curious and isolated figure, vulnerable in his solitude. He half-expects to see Reiner there.

He tries to hitch a ride but nobody will stop. There aren't many black people in cars and they barely glance at him anyway, but even the white families or couples or single women in jewels and tall hairstyles, come from Bloemfontein to the casinos for a wild night or two of gambling, glare at him with mistrust or contempt as they sail past with uptilted chins. Maybe he looks dirty or unkempt, he certainly doesn't look like them, a halo of danger rings him round. By the time it's dusk and the temperature is dropping, his despair is like another layer of clothes. There is nowhere to sleep, nowhere safe to pitch his tent, he would re-cross the border if this would help, but he'd be just as alone on the other side.

At the point when it is almost completely dark a minibus taxi comes by, the driver shouting his destination out the window, Jo'burg Jo'burg. Johannesburg is close to Pretoria, he has friends he can stay with, it's as good as home, yes please, he shouts, yes. The driver looks at him and stops. How much.

Seventy rand.

I've only got thirty.

He shakes his head. I can't help you.

Please.

Sorry.

He is starting to change gears to pull away when I say, will you take thirty rand and my watch.

The driver looks at him again, who is this mad whitey, he holds out his hand. He slips off his watch and passes it through the window. He has a suspicion the man might just pull away, what could he do to stop it, but he examines the watch and shrugs, get in.

The minibus is empty, but the driver, whose name is Paul, takes him a little way down the road to a big dead tree under which all the other passengers are waiting. He is the last one and the only white person amongst them. This is not like the taxis from the city that he's used to, where everybody mixes and is convivial, he is the odd person out here, nobody speaks to him. But Paul takes a liking to him, come and sit up in the front, he says, the road rushes blue and violent towards them through rain all the way.

At midnight he is climbing out onto a pavement in Hillbrow, the lights of the city like a heatless yellow fire around him. He shakes hands with Paul, who is driving straight back to Lesotho to pick up another load of passengers. He watches the minibus disappear, tail lights merging with all the other random moving lights, then the passengers disperse in various directions, among the crowds, lives joined together for a little while and then unjoined again.

He stays up in Pretoria for a few weeks. Only sometimes does he think of Reiner. Then he wonders where he is and what he might be doing. Somewhere in his mind he assumes that Reiner must have done what he did, walked hard and fast to get out of the mountains, and then travelled back down to Cape Town. The journey in Lesotho was one they were making together, he surely wouldn't want to continue alone.

One day, on impulse, he phones various friends down in Cape Town. He wants to know whether they've seen Reiner, has he reappeared, has he passed through. No, nobody has seen him, nobody's heard a word. But what happened, his friends want to know, what went wrong. He tries to explain but all of it clots and curdles on his tongue. Till now he hasn't had pangs of real conscience but he feels them begin when he hears the incredulity in the voice of one of these friends, that's what you did, you walked away from him in the mountains. Yes that's what happened but you don't understand.

Yes that is what happened. Now he feels exquisite agonies of unease, maybe the failure wasn't the mutual one he's constructed in his head, maybe it belongs to himself alone. If I had done this, if I had said that, in the end you are always more tormented by what you didn't do than what you did, actions already performed can always be rationalized in time, the neglected deed might have changed the world.

After about a month he goes back to Cape Town. He has no place of his own down there and must begin looking all over again. Meanwhile he stays with different friends, living in spare rooms once more, moving around. His attention has shifted from recent events to the problems of the present. He doesn't think of Reiner that often now. By this time he presumes he must be back in Germany, leading the life he was so secretive about, hating me from afar.

But Reiner appears again suddenly, without warning, one arbitrary day. During all this time, while he was up in Pretoria and then trying to resettle himself in Cape Town, Reiner was in Lesotho. He stayed committed to their project. He has lost a lot of weight, his clothes hang loosely on him, he is weak and depleted. He has spent the time walking, he says, though where he went exactly and what he did will never be revealed.

Even this much comes in second-hand, through indirect reports. Before they left he had introduced Reiner to a friend of his who was living in the same block of flats. Now this friend calls to say that Reiner arrived on his doorstep the day before, looking haggard and terrible, with nowhere to go. He wanted to know if he could stay there for a week, till his flight back home. Of course he had said yes, it's only for a few days.

He stays for three months. He sleeps on the couch in the lounge, hardly going out, barely moving around the flat at first. He's in a very bad state. He is afflicted by various illnesses with alarming symptoms, he has very high fevers, he has swollen glands, he has some kind of fungal infection on his tongue. The friend takes him to two doctors, who prescribe antibiotics. But the illnesses don't seem to clear up and Reiner shows no interest in leaving.

All of these reports come through his friend, over the telephone or in person. In the whole time that Reiner's there he never once goes over to the flat, he doesn't want to see Reiner, he doesn't want to speak to him. In truth he's shocked that he has appeared again, in his mind this episode has already been relegated to the past, this return feels almost personally directed at him. But he has a fascination with his presence so close by, he makes constant enquiries about him, he would like to know what happened since he saw him. Very little is forthcoming. But he gathers from his friend that Reiner is just as fascinated with him. He asks about me, where did I go to, where am I now. Sometimes he rails against me. Why, he wants to know, why did I storm off, things were so good between us, what got into his head.

He finds himself protesting, ask him, he knows why it happened, the friend listens sympathetically but also with doubt, he can see in his face that he has heard another version of things from Reiner, the second story unwritten here. The two stories push against each other, they will never be reconciled, he wants to argue and explain till the other story disappears.

Sometimes it feels that Reiner will never leave. He will occupy the couch in the corner of the lounge, so as to occupy a corner of his life, forever. But eventually he does gather himself together. He shakes off some of the illness, starts to eat properly, puts on a bit of weight. He goes out and about again, walking in the streets. Then money arrives for him mysteriously from overseas, and he finally confirms a date for his ticket home.

In all this time, he spends a great deal of effort and energy avoiding the German. But there are two occasions on which they run into each other. The first happens one ordinary day, in the most ordinary of places. By now he has moved into a flat on his own, not far from where Reiner is staying. He goes to the local post-office one morning to send some letters, but as he is approaching the outside entrance he has a sudden clear perception that Reiner is inside. Don't go in, he's there. He stops dead, but then he wants to know whether his premonition was correct. Of course he goes through the door and they stare at each other for the first time in months. Reiner is in the queue, waiting, and though he falters for a moment he goes to the back of the line. His heart is hammering and his palms are sweating. The queue loops back on itself at a hundred and eighty degrees and Reiner is in the other half of the line, so that the two of them are moving towards each other one place at a time. A step, a step, another step. When the next person is served they will be opposite each other, an arm away, as close as they were when lying in the tent. He wants to run but he doesn't dare.

Then Reiner turns on his heel, steps over the rope and walks out. I tremble with a weird sense of victory.

The second and last occasion is a few weeks afterwards, in the evening, in the street. He has been visiting friends and is walking back home alone. He is next to a long curved wall and he sees two people walking towards him. He realizes that the one on the outside, closest to him, is Reiner, he is with a woman he doesn't know. The woman is talking, deep in conversation, while Reiner listens, but shock registers in his body when he looks up. If they were both alone perhaps one of them would cross the street to get away, or perhaps this time they would stop to speak. Well. Hello. Hello. How are you. But the foreign presence of the woman is like a distance and a silence between them and they only watch each other as they draw slowly closer on their curved trajectory, and when they are almost level Reiner smiles. It is the old sardonic smile, saying everything by saying nothing, the corners of the mouth lifting in the rigid mask of the face, and then they pass. He doesn't look back and he is almost certain Reiner doesn't either.

Then he's gone. My friend calls to say, well, Reiner left last night, and with that single sentence the whole story is over. He waits for some further event, he doesn't know what, a phone-call, a letter, to resolve things, even though he doesn't want to make contact himself. Then at some point he realizes that the silence, the suspension, is the only form of resolution this particular story will ever have.

Maybe when two people meet for the first time all the possible variations on destiny are contained in their separate natures. These two will be drawn together, those two will be repulsed, most will pass politely with averted gaze and hurry on alone. Was what happened between him and Reiner love or hate or something else with another name. I don't know. But this is how it ends. Some time afterwards, clearing out his desk when he is moving house again, he finds the notebook in which Reiner had written his name and address years ago in Greece, and after looking at the tiny narrow handwriting for a while he throws it away. Then he takes out Reiner's letters too, a big bundle of them, and drops them into the bin. It isn't revenge and nothing else will follow on. But although he will hardly think of Reiner again, and when he does it is without regret, there are still times, walking on a country road alone, when he would not be surprised to see a dark figure in the distance, coming towards him.

TWO

THE LOVER

A few years later he is wandering in Zimbabwe. No particular reason or intention has brought him here. He decides on impulse one morning to leave, he buys a ticket in the afternoon, he gets on a bus that night. He has it in mind to travel around for two weeks and then go back.

What is he looking for, he himself doesn't know. At this remove, his thoughts are lost to me now, and yet I can explain him better than my present self, he is buried under my skin. His life is unweighted and centreless, so that he feels he could blow away at any time. He still has not made a home for himself. All his few belongings are in storage again and he has spent months in that old state of his, wandering around from one spare room to another. It has begun to feel as if he's never lived in any other way, nor will he ever settle down. Something in him has changed, he can't seem to connect properly with the world. He feels this not as a failure of the world but as a massive failing in himself, he would like to change it but doesn't know how. In his clearest moments he thinks that he has lost the ability to love, people or places or things, most of all the person and place and thing that he is. Without love nothing has value, nothing can be made to matter very much.

In this state travel isn't celebration but a kind of mourning, a way of dissipating yourself. He moves around from one place to another, not driven by curiosity but by the bored anguish of staying still. He spends a few days in Harare, then goes down to Bulawayo. He does the obligatory things required of visitors, he goes to the Matopos and sees the grave of Cecil John Rhodes, but he can't produce the necessary awe or ideological disdain, he would rather be somewhere else. If I was with somebody, he thinks, with somebody I loved, then I could love the place and even the grave too, I would be happy to be here.

He takes the overnight train to Victoria Falls. He lies in his bunk, hearing the breathing of strangers stacked above and below him, and through the window sees villages and sidings flow in out of the dark, the outlines of people and cattle and leaves stamped out in silhouette against the lonely light, then flowing backward again, out of sight into the past. Why is he happiest in moments like these, the watcher hiding in the dark. He doesn't want the sun to rise or this particular journey to end.

In the morning they come to the end of the line. He gets out with his single bag and walks to the campsite. Even early in the day the air is heavy and humid, green leaves burn with a brilliant glow. There are other travellers all around, most are younger than himself. He pitches his tent in the middle of the camp and goes down to look at the falls.

It is incredible to see the volume and power of so much water endlessly dropping into the abyss, but part of him is elsewhere, somewhere higher up and to the right, looking down at an angle not only on the falls but on himself there, among the crowds. This part of him, the part that watches, has been here for a while now, and it never quite goes away, over the next few days it looks at him keeping busy, strolling through the streets from one curio-shop to another, going for long walks in the surrounding bush, it observes with amazement when he goes white-water rafting on the river, it sees him lying in the open next to his tent to keep cool at night, staring up into the shattered windscreen of the sky. And though he seems content, though he talks to people and smiles, the part that watches isn't fooled, it knows he wants to move on.

On the third or fourth day he goes for a swim at one of the hotel pools. Afterwards he sits at a table near the bar to have a drink and his attention is slowly drawn to a group of young people nearby. They all have their rucksacks with them, they are about to depart. They're a strange mixture, a bit uneasy with each other, a plump Englishman with his girlfriend, a blond Danish man, two younger dark girls who sit close together, not speaking. He recognizes a burly Irish woman who went rafting with him two days ago, and goes over to speak to her. Where are you all off to.

Malawi. We're going through Zambia. Maybe she sees something in my face, because after a moment she asks, do you want to come along.

He sits thinking for a few moments, then says, I'll be right back.

He runs madly from the hotel to the campsite and takes down his tent. When he gets back he sits among his new companions, panting, feeling edgy with doubt. Soon afterwards the man they're waiting for, an Australian called Richard, arrives, and they all stir themselves to leave. He has gathered already that these people don't know each other well, they have banded together by chance to make this journey safely. Hence the unease. He doesn't mind, in fact the general mood suits him, he doesn't feel a pressure to fit in. With the others he loads his bag onto the back of an open van and climbs up. They have paid somebody to drive them to the other side of the border.

It's getting dark when they arrive at the station. They are late and the queue for tickets is long, they can only get third-class seats, sitting amongst a crowd in an open carriage in which all the lights are broken. Almost before they can find a place the train lurches and starts to move.

There is a moment when any real journey begins. Sometimes it happens as you leave your house, sometimes it's a long way from home.

I n the dark there is the sound of breaking glass and a voice cries out. They have been travelling for perhaps an hour, the darkness in the carriage is total, but now somebody lights a match. In the guttering glow he sees a hellish scene, on one of the seats further down a man clutches his bloodied face, a pool of blood on the floor around him, rocking from side to side with the violent motion of the train. Everybody shrinks away, the light goes out. What's happening, the Irish girl says to him.

What's happening is that somebody has thrown a rock through the window. Almost immediately it comes again, the smashing glass, the cry, but this time nobody is hurt, the cry is one of fear. They are all afraid, and with good reason, because every time the train passes some town or settlement there is the noise, the cry, or the deep thudding sound of the rock hitting the outside of the train. Everybody sits hunched forward with their arms over their heads.

Late in the night the ordeal winds down. Inside the train the mood becomes lighter, people who would otherwise never have spoken strike up conversations. Somebody takes out bandages for those who've been hurt. At the far end of the carriage are three women travelling with little babies, their window has been broken and the wind is howling through, do you mind, they ask, if we come and sit with you. Not at all. He is with the Irish woman on a seat, the rest of their group is elsewhere, they move up to make space. Now the dark smells warm and yeasty, there is a sucking and gurgling all around. The women are travelling to Lusaka for a church conference on female emancipation, they have left their husbands behind, but a couple of them are holding a child and the other woman has triplets. She is sitting opposite him, he can see her in the passing lights from outside. Now a weird scenario begins. The triplets are all identically dressed in white bunny suits, she starts to breast-feed them two at a time. The third one she hands to him, would you mind, no not at all, he holds the murmuring weight in his hands. Occasionally she changes them over, he hands on a little bunnysuited baby and receives an exact copy in exchange, this seems to go on for hours. Sometimes one of her nipples comes free, a baby cries, then she says, please could you, the Irish woman leans over to rearrange her breast, sucking starts again. The women talk softly to the white travellers and among themselves, and sometimes they sing hymns.

By the next morning his head is fractured with fatigue and swirling with bizarre images. Under the cold red sky of dawn Lusaka is another surreal sight, shanty towns sprouting between the buildings, tin and plastic and cardboard hemmed in by brick and glass. They climb out among crowds onto the platform. The three women say goodbye and go off with their freight of babies to discuss their liberation. While he waits for the little group to gather he looks off to one side and sees, further down the train, at the second class compartments, another little group of white travellers disembarking. Three of them, a woman and two men. He watches but the crowds close around him.

They walk to the bus-station through streets filled with early light and litter blowing aimlessly. Somebody has a map and knows which way to go. Even at this hour, five or six in the morning, the place is full of people standing idly and staring. They are the focus of much ribald curiosity, he's glad he's not alone. On one corner an enormous bearded man steps forward and, with the perfunctory disinterest with which one might weigh fruit, squeezes the Irish woman's left breast in his hand. She hits his fingers away. You not in America now, the man shouts after them, I fuck you all up.

The bus-station is a mad chaos of engines and people under a metal roof, but they eventually find their bus. When they get on the first people he sees are the three white travellers from the train, sitting in a row, very quietly looking ahead of them, and as he passes they don't look up. The woman and the one man are young, in their early twenties, and the other man is older, perhaps his own age. He passes them and takes a seat at the very back of the bus. The rest of his group is scattered around. He hasn't interacted or spoken with them much, and at the moment he's more interested in the other three travellers a few rows ahead, he can see the backs of their heads. Who are they, what are they doing here, how do they fit together.

It takes eight hours to get to the border. They disembark into the main square of a little town, where taxi drivers clamour to take them to the actual border post. While they're negotiating a price he sees from the corner of his eye the three travellers get into a separate car and leave. They're not at the border post when he gets there, they must have gone through. There is a press of people, a long wait, by the time their passports have been stamped and the taxi has driven them on through the ten kilometres or so of noman's land it is getting dark.

When he enters the Malawian border post, a white building under trees, some kind of dispute is in progress. A uniformed official is shouting at the three travellers, who look confused, you must have a visa, you must have a visa. The older man, the one his own age, is trying to explain. His English is good, but hesitant and heavily accented. The embassy told us, he says. The embassy told you the wrong thing, the uniformed official shouts, you must have a visa. What must we do. Go back to Lusaka. They look at him and then confer among themselves. The official has lost interest, he turns to the new arrivals, give me your passports. South Africans don't need visas, he is stamped through. He pauses for a second, then goes up to the three. Where are you from.

I am French. It's the older man speaking. They are from Switzerland. He points to the other two, whose faces are now as neutral as masks, not understanding or not wanting to talk.

Do you want me to speak to him for you.

No. It's okay. Thank you. He has thick curly hair and round glasses and a serious expression which is impassive, or perhaps merely resigned. The younger man has from up close a beauty that is almost shocking, red lips and high cheek-bones and a long fringe of hair. His brown eyes won't meet my gaze.

What will you do now.

I don't know. He shrugs.

They languish for a few days in Lilongwe, a feature-less town full of white expatriates and jacaranda trees, killing time while somebody in their party tries to organize a visa to go somewhere. He is bored and frustrated, and by now he is irritated with the other travellers in the group. They are completely content to sit around drinking beer for hours, they go out in search of loud music at night, and some of them show an unpleasant disdain for the poverty they encounter. The two young women in particular, who turn out to be Swedish, have stopped being silent and go on in loud voices about their terrible trip through Zambia. The rocks, oh, it was just horrible, and the bus-station, oh, it was so dirty, it smelled, oh, disgusting. The shortcomings and squalor of the continent have let them down personally, it never seems to occur to them that the conditions they found horrible and dis-gusting are not part of a set that will be struck when they have gone offstage.

But things improve a little when they get to the lake. It's the destination he's had in mind since leaving Zimbabwe, everything he's ever heard about Malawi has been centred on that long body of water running up half the length of the country. Take a look at him there a few days later, standing on the beach at Cape Maclear. He is staring at the water with an amazed expression, as if he can't believe how beau-tiful it is. Light glitters on the tilting surface, the blond mountains seem almost colourless next to the intense blue of the water, a cluster of islands rise up a kilometre from the shore. A wooden canoe passes slowly in perfect profile, like a hieroglyph.

As the day goes on his wonder only grows, the water is smooth and warm to swim in, under the surface are schools of brightly coloured tropical fish, there is nothing to do except lie on the sand in the sun and watch fishermen repairing their nets. The pace of everything here is slow and unhurried, the only sound of an engine is from the occasional car on the dirt road high up.

Even the local people take up their appointed place in this version of paradise, they are happy to drop everything when called and go out fishing for these foreign visitors, or prepare a meal on the beach for them in the evening and clean up when they're gone. They will row you out to the islands for the price of a cool drink, or go running for miles over the hot sand to fetch some of the famous Malawi cob, even carving you a wooden pipe to smoke it in. When they're not needed they simply fade into the background, going back to their natural tasks, supplying peaceful lines of smoke from the picturesque huts they live in, or heading across your line of vision at an appropriate moment in the distance.

Only someone cold and hard of heart could fail to succumb to these temptations, the idea of travelling, of going away, is an attempt to escape time, mostly the attempt is futile, but not here, the little waves lap at the shores just as they always have done, the rhythms of daily life are dictated by the larger ones of nature, the sun or moon for example, something has lasted here from the mythical place before history set itself in motion, ticking like a bomb. It would be easy to just stop and not start again, and indeed a lot of people have done that, you can see them if you take a little walk, here and there at various points on the beach are gatherings that haven't moved in months. Talk to them and they'll tell you about themselves, Sheila from Bristol, Jürgen from Stuttgart, Shlomo from Tel Aviv, they've been here half a year, a year, two years, they all have the glazed halfshaven look of lethargy, or is it dope. This is the best place in the world, they say, stick around you'll see, you can survive on next to nothing, a bit of money sent from home once in a while, we'll go back again one day of course but not just yet.

And already after a day, two days, three, the massive gravity of inertia sets in, the effort of walking from your room to the water is already more than it seems necessary to expend. Swim, sleep, smoke. The people he came here with can't believe their luck. This is the real Africa to them, the one they came from Europe to find, not the fake expensive one dished up to them at Victoria Falls, or the dangerous frightening one that tried to hurt them on the train. In this place each of them is at the centre of the universe, and at the same time is nowhere, surely this is what it means to be spiritually fulfilled, they are having a religious experience.

And at first he himself partakes of it, look at him now, lying on the beach and then getting up and stumbling to the water for a swim. Later when he's too hot he goes back to his room to sleep, or retreats to the bar for a drink. When a joint is passed around he puffs along with everybody else, his face relaxes into the same befuddled grin that makes everyone around him look stupid. He's as hedonistic as the rest of them. Towards evening he wanders with some of the others in the group, they are all talking and laughing like old friends, to a clearing behind the village where some bearded itinerant hippie is offering sunset flights in a micro-light. Although he won't go up he watches Richard ascend for a long looping meandering cruise above the lake, and the gentle suspension of the little machine in the last light contains something of the unreal weightlessness of being here.

But the truth is that even in the first sybaritic day or two there is that same blue thread of uneasiness in him, no amount of heat or marijuana will quite sedate the restlessness. He is outside the group, observing. They have been around each other now for long enough for connections and tensions to develop, they all carry on like old companions. Everybody is called by nicknames, there is a lot of laughter and joking. Between Richard and the Irish woman a romance has sprung up, one evening on the beach he notices them shifting closer to each other, smiling coyly and watching one another sidelong, shortly afterwards they retire to Richard's room nearby and emerge later glowing warmly. It's all touching and happy, but he's the odd one out here, he keeps a distance between himself and them, no matter how friendly they are. Once when all of them are walking on the beach he listens to a conversation behind him, one of the Swedish girls is talking to the Danish man, how did you like South Africa when you were there, oh, he says in reply, the country was beautiful, if only all the South Africans weren't so fucked-up. Then everyone becomes aware of him at once and silence falls, of all of them he is the only one smiling, but inwardly.

Then one day someone in their party has this wonderful idea, let's hire a boat and go out to that island for the day. One of the local men is conscripted to row them there for a small fee, over which the plump Englishman haggles, he will let them use his goggles and flippers to go snorkelling with. These are among the few things he owns, the boat and oars, the mask and flippers, but while he rows he talks earnestly about how he is saving to go to medical school in South Africa, he would like to be a doctor. He's a young man of twenty three with a wide gentle face and a body toned and hardened by fishing for a living. Nobody else in the party is interested in speaking to him, but he tells me later, on the island, about how they go night-fishing, rowing for miles and miles into the far deep centre of the lake, each boat with a torch burning in the prow, and how they row back at dawn weighed down by a pyramid of fish. Would you take me with you one night, I would like to see that. Yes, I will take you.

Through glass the bottom of the lake is the surface of an alien planet, huge boulders are piled on each other in the sun-lit depths, glowing fish float and dart like birds. The day is long and languid and everybody is happy when at last they climb into the boat to be rowed back again. But their oarsman is looking around, worried. What's the matter. One of the flip-pers has gone. The visitors sigh and chatter in the boat, while I get out to help him look. The price of the flipper is worth maybe a week or two of fishing to this man. We search in the shallow water, between the crevices in the rocks. Hurry up, one of the Swedish girls calls crossly, we're waiting for you. But now the anger finally touches the surface of his tongue, you get out of there, he cries, his voice rising, get out of there and help us look. One of you has lost the flipper, we're not going back till you find it again. There is muttering and resentment, let him buy a new one, but they all troop out onto the shore and pretend to cast around. In the end the flipper is found and everybody gets back into the boat and in a little while the friv-olous conversation resumes, but he knows that his outburst has confirmed what they suspect, he is not the same as them, he is a fucked-up South African.

Something has changed for him now, he finds it difficult to make innocent conversation with these people. The next day he goes off alone on a long walk down the beach. At the far end, where the local village is, where the tourists never go, is a rocky headland, he thinks he would like to climb round it. But when he gets there he discovers that people have shat among the rocks, everywhere he tries to climb he finds old smelly turds and wreaths of paper. He can imagine the shrill voices of the Swedish

girls, oh how disgusting, and it is, but now another notion comes
to him, that if people are using these rocks for a toilet it's
because they don't have an alternative. He climbs back down,
his head hurting, his feet in pain on the hot sand. Nearby there
is some kind of marina for wealthy expatriates, expensive yachts
lift their silken sails like standards, but he passes it by and goes
into the village. He tells himself he's doing it for the cool of the
shade between the huts, but really a curiosity drives him. On the
long hot walk back to his room he sees properly for the first time
the ragged clothes on the smiling children, the bare interiors of
the smoky huts with their two or three pieces of broken furniture, the skeletal dogs slinking away at his approach, and for
the first time he chooses to understand why people who live
here, whose country this is, might want to run errands for these
foreign visitors passing through, and catch fish and cook for
them, and clean up after them. It may only be the heat but his
headache is very bad, and through the haze of pain the beautiful landscape has receded and broken into disparate elements,
the water here, the mountain there, the horizon in another
place again, and all of these into their constituent parts too, a
series of shapes and textures and lines that have nothing to do
with him.

When he gets back the Irish girl is sitting outside her room
in the courtyard, smoking a cigarette. I'm feeling upset, she
tells him, I just lost my temper with somebody, I think I was a
bit extreme. The person she lost her temper with is an old man
who works at the guest-house, she paid him, she says, to do her
washing for her, but when he'd finished he hung it up on the
line and neglected to take it down and fold it. Is it too much to
expect, she wonders aloud, when you pay somebody to do
your washing that they should fold it when it's dry. She smiles
and asks, did I go too far.

He can't contain it any more, the anger that fuelled his little outburst yesterday is now a rage. Yes, he tells her, you went too far. She looks startled and confused. But why. Because he's an old man maybe three times your age. Because he lives here, this is his home, and you're a visitor. Because you're lucky enough to have the money to pay this old man to wash your clothes, your dirty underwear, while you lie around on the beach, you ought to feel ashamed of yourself instead of being so certain that you're right.

He says all of this without raising his voice but he sounds choked and vehement, he himself is startled at how furious he is. She blinks and seems about to cry, such anger for such a little thing, but his anger is not just at her or even at the others in their party, the hottest part of it is for himself. He is as guilty as any of them, he too is passing through, he too has luck and money, all his self-righteousness will not absolve him. After she has gone scurrying off he sits in the twilight outside his room, while his anger cools into misery. Even before she comes back to tell him that she went to the old man and apologized, so everything is all right now, he knows that the spell is broken and he can't be one of the lotus-eaters any more, he has to move on, move on.

He leaves the next morning early, as the sun is coming up. Everything is fixed and still in the glassy air, the mountains of Mozambique are visible across the turquoise water of the lake. Talking to the man at the front desk of the guest-house last night, he learned that a ferry will be leaving from Monkey Bay this morning, going up the whole length of the lake. This sounds good to him, he'll travel north to some other town where nobody knows him. He waits up on the dirt road for the bus.

When he gets to Monkey Bay the ferry is already at the dock, a rusting agglomeration of metal listing badly to one side. He buys a ticket to Nkhata Bay, halfway up the lake. There is a small crowd of passengers, mostly local people with crates and boxes.

When the boat starts to move he goes and stands at the rail, in a little while he sees the islands of Cape Maclear floating by. It feels good to be alone in the cool early morning on the lake. After an hour or so the ferry moves in towards the shore again and docks at Salima, where passengers get off and on. He waits till they move out into the middle of the lake again before he starts to wander around. The boat is a whole little world on its own, with passages and stairs and limits and rules, and a slowly increasing population. He stops to watch a crowd pressing in on the hatch where food is served. There are limbs and feet and faces moving, all anonymous and tangled, but when he glances to one side they are standing there. The three travellers from the bus. Where have you been.

They have been back to Lusaka to get their visas. They have had a terrible time. They managed to get a lift with a local man, who was very keen to take them in his car. It turned out that somebody had been using this car to sleep in in the bush and had been murdered in it two nights before, so the back seat was covered in dried blood on which two of them had to perch for the whole long drive. They got to Lusaka on Friday afternoon to discover that the Malawian embassy was closed till Monday, so they sat around in a hotel room to wait. Now they have their visas and are not stopping to linger, they are trying to get up to Tanzania as soon as they can, from where they are hoping to find a boat or a cheap flight that will take them back to Europe. Two of them, the two men, have been travelling in Africa for a long time, nine months or more, and they are eager to get home.

All this he finds out in little bits and pieces through the day. Soon after he meets up with them, they come out to join him on the front deck. The boat is filling up at every stop and the only way to claim a place is to put your bag down somewhere. Sitting out there in the sun, chatting idly, he discovers that the Swiss travellers are twins. Their names are Alice and Jerome. The Frenchman, Christian, is the only one at all fluent in English. It's through him that most conversation goes. He tells me that he and Jerome met each other in Mauritania and went on from there through Senegal, Guinea and Mali to the Ivory Coast, from where they flew to South Africa.

They have been there a couple of months, in which time Alice joined them, and now they're on their way home.

Jerome listens attentively to this account, and now and then he interjects in French with a question or a comment. But when I ask him something, his face stiffens in confusion and he turns to the others for help.

He doesn't understand, Christian says. Ask me.

So the question has to be repeated to Christian, who translates it, and then translates the reply. The same happens in reverse when Jerome questions me, we look at each other but speak to Christian. This gives the whole conversation a weird formality, through which no personal quality can break. I can never ask what I would like to, what is your relationship with

Christian, what bond has kept you going all the way from West Africa. Once the most basic facts have been exchanged there seems nothing more to say.

Later in the day a wind comes up and the surface of the lake turns choppy. Then the ship starts to pitch and roll, drawing a thin line of queasiness under everything. When the sun goes down it turns suddenly very cold. He is on the other side of the raised middle section of the deck to them, lying head to head with Jerome, and as he settles himself for the night he rolls his eyes up and finds Jerome in exactly the same position, looking back, and for a long arrested moment they hold each other's gaze before they both look away and try to sleep.

In fact he doesn't sleep much, the boat is lurching and the deck is hard and uncomfortable. Dangling above them is a huge metal hook on a crane and all his latent uneasiness becomes focused on this hook, what if it comes loose, what if it falls, he keeps waking from jagged dreams to see that dark shape punched out on the sky. The night is starry and huge, despite this one concentration of dread at the very centre of it, above him.

In the morning all the bodies stagger up stiffly from the deck, yawning and rubbing their necks. It takes a long time for conversation to start up, but even when everybody around him is talking he doesn't much feel like words today. He is tired and sore and looking forward to being on land again. They dock at Nkhata Bay soon afterwards. By now the heat is already build-ing and he doesn't envy them the long voyage to the north, they will only arrive tomorrow. He says goodbye on the deck and this time he knows he won't see them again. He gets off in a dense press of bodies, the ship's horn bellows mournfully.

He shoulders his pack and sets out in the hot sun, heading to a guest-house ten kilometres out of town. By the time he finds the place a few hours have gone by. The setting is lovely, a series of communal bamboo houses on stilts along the edge of the beach. He lays out his sleeping bag at one end of a row of others and changes into shorts and goes out for a swim. He leaves his towel on the beach and swims far out into the lake. The waves are strong and rough here, by the time he comes back to shore he feels replenished and renewed.

Jerome, Alice and Christian are standing next to his towel, grinning. Hello, they say. It's us again.

T hey changed their minds at the last moment and decided to get off the boat. They thought they would rest here for a day or two and then continue overland. They are staying in a bungalow at the far end of the beach, half-hidden among trees.

He spends that day with them on the beach. All their towels are laid out in a row, they drift in and out of the water or sprawl in the sun. He gives himself completely to the pagan pleasures of idleness and heat, what wasn't possible for him with the other travellers down south is perfectly possible here, but underneath his tan he feels troubled. The way in which this mysterious threesome has threaded through his journey bothers him, there is almost the shape of a design to it, in which none of them has a say. Like this little reunion, for instance, it's purely by chance that they've also come to stay at this place, if they'd taken a room in town they would probably not have seen each other again. Or perhaps he wants to see it like this, it's only human, after all, to look for a hint of destiny where love or longing is concerned.

He is never alone with Jerome. Once or twice, when Christian has gone off to swim and Alice gets up to join him, it seems he and Jerome will be the only ones left there on the sand. But it doesn't happen. Christian appears at the last moment, coming up dripping and panting from the lake, throwing himself down on his towel. But if he's laying claim to the younger man he doesn't show it, in fact it's Christian who suggests, sometime in that day or in the one following, that he come along with them to Tanzania. If you feel like it, why not, it will be fun. All of them seem pleased at the thought, there is no resentment or reluctance. Well, he says, I might, let me think about that.

He does have to think about it, the answer isn't simple. Apart from the complications of the situation, which will only thicken and grow, there are practical questions to be considered, he meant only to visit Zimbabwe, now he's in Malawi, does he want to go on to Tanzania. While he tries to make up his mind, he continues to pass the days with the three of them at the lake edge. It is a restful time, the substance of it made of warmth and moving liquid and grains of sand, everything standing still and at the same time pouring and flowing. At the centre of it, the only solid object, is Jerome, lying on his side in his shorts, skin beaded with water, or throwing his hair back out of his eyes, or diving into the waves. He has become relaxed with me now, the questions he sometimes flings out at me through Christian have become more personal in nature. What do you do. Where do you live. But even here he is outside the group, looking in. In the way the three of them talk and joke and gesture there is also the weight of a private history that will always be impervious to him. Things have happened between them that he can never be party to, so that their lives have become subtly joined. Even if he could speak French he could never close up the gap. This sets him apart, making his loneliness resound in him with a high thin note, like the lingering sound of a bell.

In the evenings they eat their meals together in the restaurant at the top of the hill, after which they say goodnight and go their separate ways. Then he sits alone on the top step outside the hut and watches the lights of canoes in a long row far out. Lightning flares above the lake, like the signature of God.

On the evening of the second day, or is it the third, when they say goodnight on the beach Christian mentions in an offhand way that they will be leaving in the morning. They are taking a bus up to Karonga in the north, and going to Tanzania the next day. Almost as an afterthought he adds, have you decided, are you interested in coming.

He finds himself taking the same tone, his voice surprises him by its flatness. Hmm, he says, yes, I think I will come with you. I'll go as far as the border and see if they'll let me in.

I n the crowd waiting for the bus the next morning is another white traveller, a thin man with black hair and an unconvincing moustache, wearing jeans and a loud purple shirt. After a while he comes sauntering over.

Where are you going.

To Tanzania.

Ah. Me too. He smiles toothily under his moustache. Me, I am from Santiago. In Chile.

They shake hands. The newcomer's name is Roderigo, he's been working in Mozambique but now he's on his way up to Kenya, somebody has told him that there are cheap flights from Nairobi to India, where for some reason he wants to go before he returns home. He volunteers all this information in the forthright way some people have on the road, he has the melancholy of certain travellers who want to cling, and though nobody feels especially drawn to him they allow him to drift into the group.

By the time they get to Karonga, far to the north, they are all quiet and withdrawn, the air is smoky with twilight. The bus-station is at the edge of town and they have to walk in with their packs along the drab main road. They take a while to find a place to stay. Karonga is nothing like the villages down south, it's big and unappealing with that quality of border towns, of transitoriness and traffic and a slightly scuffed danger, even though the border is still sixty kilometres away. In the end they find two rooms in an inn on an untarred back street, the place is made of concrete and filthy inside, the bathrooms furred over with mould. The ugliness stirs a sadness in him, which grows when he is left in one room on his own.

He has always had a dread of crossing borders, he doesn't like to leave what's known and safe for the blank space beyond in which anything can happen. Everything at times of transition takes on a symbolic weight and power. But this too is why he travels. The world you're moving through flows into another one inside, nothing stays divided any more, this stands for that, weather for mood, landscape for feeling, for every object there is a corresponding inner gesture, everything turns into metaphor. The border is a line on a map, but also drawn inside himself somewhere.

But in the morning everything is different, even the mud streets have a sort of rough charm. They hitch a lift to the border and go through the Malawian formalities together. Then they walk across a long bridge over a choked green riverbed to the immigration post on the other side.

It's only now that he starts to really consider what might happen. Although he'd said airily that he'd see if they would let him in, it didn't seriously occur to him that they might not. But now, as the little cluster of sheds draws closer, with a boom across the road on the far side, a faint premonition prickles in his palms, maybe this won't turn out as he hopes. And once they have entered the first wooden shed, and all the others have been stamped through by the dapper little man behind his counter, his passport is taken from him and in the pause that follows, the sudden stillness of the hand as it reaches for the ink, he knows what's coming. Where is your visa. I didn't know I needed one. You do.

That is all. The passport is folded closed and returned to him.

What can I do.

The little man shrugs. He is neat and compact and clean, his chin impeccably shaven. Nothing you can do.

Isn't there a consulate somewhere.

Not in Malawi. He turns away to tend to other people, people flowing in and out of the border, people who don't need visas.

The little group gathers sadly outside. Cicadas are shrieking on some impossible frequency, like a gang of mad dentists drilling in the treetops. The metal roof is humming in the heat. They feel bad on his behalf, he can see it in their faces, but he doesn't want to meet their eyes. He sits down on a step to wait while they go next door to the health office and customs. He can't quite believe this is happening. In a sudden flurry of emotion he gets up, goes back inside.

I heard of somebody who visited Tanzania, he says. A South African. He didn't need a visa, he got a stamp here.

Where this memory has come from I don't know, but it's true, I did meet such a person. The man's eyebrows go up. And what did he pay, he says, for this stamp.

He is stupefied. He doesn't know what the man paid, he doesn't know what it has to do with anything. He shakes his head.

Then I can't help you.

Again he turns away to help somebody else. Vibrating with anguish and alarm, he waits for the little man to finish, please, he says, please.

I told you. I can't help you.

Everything that he desires in the world at this moment lies in a space beyond this obtuse and efficient public servant whom he will do anything, anything, to overthrow. What is your name, he says.

You want my name. The man shakes his head and sighs, his face has yet to yield up an expression, he pulls a black ledger across the counter towards him and opens it. Your passport please.

Now hope flickers briefly, he saw the names of the others inscribed in a big book too, he gives over his passport. When his name and number have been written down he asks, what is that for.

You have been refused entry, the little man says, giving his passport back to him, this is the list of names of people who may not enter Tanzania.

What is your name, he says, you can't treat me like this. He hears the idiocy of the threat even as he makes it, who would he report this man to and for what, there is nothing he can do, in the world of metaphor and in the real world too he has arrived at a line he cannot cross. He goes back out into the sun, where the others are waiting, commiserative, did you talk to him again, what did he say. No, it's no good, I can't come with you. They stand around in the aimless awkwardness of sympathy, but already they're casting their eyes towards the road and rocking from foot to foot, it's past the middle of the day.

We'd better go, Christian says. I'm sorry.

They write down each other's addresses. The only piece of paper he has is an old bank statement, he gives it to each of them in turn. Now years later as I write this it lies in front of me on my desk, folded and creased and grubby, carrying its little cargo of names, its different sets of handwriting, some kind of impression of that instant pushed into the paper and fixed there.

He walks with them to the boom across the road. He may not go further than this. On the other side are flocks of young boys on bicycles, waiting to ferry passengers the six kilometres to the nearest town, where other transport begins. This is where they have to say goodbye. He looks down at his shoes. He finds it difficult to speak.

Have a good journey, he says eventually.

Where will you go now.

I think I'll go home. I've had enough.

Jerome says, you will come in Switzerland, yes.

The last word is a question, he answers with a nod, yes I will.

Then they are gone, climbing onto the bikes, wobbling tentatively into motion and speeding away, such a surreal departure, he stands staring but none of them looks back. Roderigo's shirt is the last vivid trace of them, the flag of the usurper, the stranger who came to take his place. Meanwhile other boys on bikes are crowding around him, blocking his view, let me take you sir you want a lift me sir me. No, he says, I'm not going with them. He looks down the road a last time, then shoulders his bag and turns. The bridge is long and lonely in the midday heat. He walks.

When he gets back to the Malawian side he finds himself dealing with the same white-uniformed official who stamped him through. There is a second or two of confusion before the man works it out, weren't you here half an hour ago.

Yes, they won't let me through. They say I need a visa. I don't have one.

The man looks at his passport, looks at him, then beckons him closer. Offer him money, he says.

What.

That's what he wants. A little bit of money. Who did you speak to.

A small guy. Very neat.

Yes, I know him, he's a friend of mine. Offer him money.

He stares back at the man, beginning to understand the conversation he had on the other side of the bridge. That cryptic statement, what did he pay for this stamp, suddenly makes sense, how could he not have seen. I am a fool, he thinks, and not only because of that.

I was nasty to him, he says. Things turned unpleasant.

But this man is losing interest too, he opens his palms and shrugs. I go back outside and stand in the sun for a long suspended moment while various possibilities arc past and return. With every second Jerome and Alice and Christian are getting further and further away, even if the little man lets him through is he going to try to catch up with them, they could be anywhere by now. But when he turns and looks back into Malawi, down the long blue road shimmering away into the distance, the prospect of retracing his steps seems just as impossible. He feels as if he'll never move again.

Then suddenly he is running over the bridge, his pack jouncing on his back. When he comes to the shed he is pouring sweat and panting, please, he says, there is something I remembered.

The little man seems unsurprised to see him. His attention is on the starched cuffs of his shirt.

The South African I told you about. The one who got the stamp. I just remembered what he paid.

No. The tidy little head shakes sadly. Your name is in the book. When your name is in the book it can't come out.

Twenty dollars.

No.

Thirty.

I thought you wanted my name. I thought you wanted to report me.

I made a mistake. I was upset. I'm very sorry about it. I apologize.

You were rude to me. It is a pity. You said you wanted my name.

I said I was sorry.

I am also sorry. It is not possible.

The circular discussion goes on and on. He feels as if he is doing battle with some mythical doorkeeper whom he has to overcome, but he doesn't have the right weapons or words. After a while another man comes in, also in uniform, but completely unlike the first man, this one is slovenly and unkempt, chewing a stick between his teeth. Hello hello hello, he says, what's the problem here.

No problem. We're just talking.

I'm the boss here, talk to me.

He looks warily at the new man. He has a gun and hand-cuffs on his belt and the sort of hearty bonhomie that might conceal a zealous devotion to duty. He ought to be careful, but there isn't time. He clears his throat. I don't have a visa, he says, but I need to get into Tanzania. Can you help me.

Now a long conversation ensues between these two officials, in which the black book is opened and examined, his passport is perused, much deliberation goes back and forth. Every word of their two encounters, it seems, is being repeated and examined. At the end of this process the boss man starts to upbraid him. You have been rude to my friend. You have upset him.

I apologized to him. I said I was sorry.

Say it again.

My friend, I'm sorry for being rude. I wasn't thinking.

That's better, the boss man says. Now everybody is polite.

His name, indelibly inscribed in the great black book, is crossed out, and all things become possible again. Now that the door is opening at last, he is frantic to catch up. But neither of these two men is prepared to rush, they must see to the details at their own leisurely pace. The boss in particular wants to explain the ethics of this transaction to him, if you want a man to break the law, he says, if you want him to risk his job, then you must make it worthwhile for this man.

Forty dollars makes it worthwhile.

The rest of the informalities are concluded, have you got a yellow fever vaccination, a cholera vaccination, no, then don't go to the health office, just pass through. The stamp you're getting isn't a visa, it's an entry stamp, so you're not legal, if you get caught it's your own problem, all right. All right. Come, I'll walk with you over the border.

In the end both of them come to see him off, standing at the boom like a pair of friendly relatives, waving. Have a nice time. Instantly the flocks of bicycle boys are around him, take me sir, me sir, take me. He chooses one who looks sturdy and strong. I have to try to catch my friends, I'll pay you double if you go as fast as you can. Yes sir, very fast. He climbs on, the boy has wired an extra seat onto the cross-bar for himself, they go toiling down the road.

It was Christian's plan, he knows, to catch a bus to Mbeya, a town about three hours away, from where there is a train to Dar es Salaam tonight. He has to find them before they leave, in the big city he will never see them again. He still has hopes that they might be waiting to catch the bus. Faster, he calls to the pedalling boy, can't you go faster. The scene feels bizarre. There are bicycles going in both directions, some with passengers, some without. The road goes up and down between green rolling hills, the sun beats down. The boy works frantically, pouring sweat, and every now and then turns his head to blow a jet of snot out of his nose. Sorry, he calls back over his shoulder. Don't be sorry, just go faster.

But when they come to the first little town the roadside is bare and deserted. He gets down and looks around, as if they might be hiding nearby. Where are my friends, he asks, but the boy shakes his head and grins. The friends of this peculiar man are no concern of his.

So he waits for the next bus to come. It's as if he's arrived at a place outside time, in which only he feels its lack. He paces up and down, he throws pebbles at a tree, he watches a file of ants going into a hole in the ground, all in a bid to summon time again. When the interval is over perhaps an hour and a half has passed. By then a small crowd is swelling next to the road and everybody clambers on board the bus at once. He ends up without a seat and has to hang on to roof racks in the aisle. Outside there is a mountainous green country-side quilted with tea plantations. Banana trees clap their broad leaves in applause.

It's a full three hours or more before the road begins to descend from this high hilly country and the edges of Mbeya accrete around him. By now the sun is setting and in the dwindling light all he can see are low, sinister buildings, made mostly of mud, crouching close to the ground. He climbs down at the edge of a crowded street swirling with fumes. He asks a woman nearby, do you know where the station is. Somebody else overhears him and repeats it to somebody else, and he finds himself escorted by a stranger to a group of men loitering nearby. He saw them when he got off the bus, an expressionless and hard-looking bunch wearing caps and dark glasses, exuding menace. One of them says that he will take him to the station for five dollars. He hesitates for a few seconds in renewed panic, he's afraid of this man in dark glasses whose car, he sees, has dark windows too, is he really going to drive off into these anonymous streets walled in by so much dark glass. But he's come this far and he doesn't know what else to do.

The man drives very fast in complete silence and then pulls up in front of a long building that is completely in darkness. By now it's night. There is a chain on the front door and not a living soul in sight. Five dollars, the man says.

I want you to wait for me. I might need a lift somewhere else.

The man waits, brooding and watchful, while he fumbles his way up and down the length of the building, calling and knocking. Eventually he finds a window behind which a light is burning. He raps and raps on the glass until somebody comes, peering out suspiciously at him.

Yes.

Excuse me. Is there a train to Dar es Salaam tonight.

Not tonight. In the morning. It's dangerous around here. You should go back into town. Come in the morning.

He returns to the car and his surly driver, could you drive me into town. I'll give you another five dollars.

The man takes him to a hotel close to the point at which he got off the bus. You're lucky, the woman at the desk tells him, you've got the last room. But he doesn't feel lucky at all as he sits on the edge of the bed, staring at the various shades of brown and beige that surround him. He can't remember when he last felt so alone. He decides that he will return to the station in the morning. If he doesn't find them there he will go back home. With this much resolved he tries to sleep, but he tosses and turns, he wakes continually into his strange surroundings to stare at a weird patch of light on the wall. At dawn he dresses and leaves the key in the door.

Opposite the hotel is an open patch of ground where the taxi rank is. As he comes to the bottom of the driveway he sees Jerome and Christian getting into a taxi. He stops dead still and then he starts to run.

T he reunion is delighted all round, lots of clamour and slapping of shoulders. In the space of five minutes the whole world has changed shape, this town that looked mean and threatening to him is suddenly full of vibrancy and life.

They go by taxi to the station. This building too is no longer the empty darkened mausoleum of last night, it's been transformed into a crowded public space filled with noise and commotion. Their train has been delayed and while they wait he goes for a long walk with Roderigo into the surrounding streets to find something to drink. A rusted Coca-Cola sign takes them into the dusty inner courtyard of a house, where they are served under a faded beach umbrella at a plastic table while chickens peck around their feet. Roderigo is still wearing his purple shirt, with a gaudy scarf tied around his neck. While we sip our drinks he tells me a story about my country. Before he went to work in Mozambique, he says, he stayed in South Africa for a few weeks, living in a hostel in Johannesburg. One day a young American traveller arrived and was put into the same room with him and they became friendly. On the second or third night Roderigo and this American went out drinking and landed up much later in a bar in Yeoville, very drunk. Roderigo wanted to go home to bed, but the American had started speaking to a black man he'd just met, who invited him to go somewhere else for another drink. The American was full of sentiment and goodwill about the country, talking to Roderigo about racial harmony and the healing of the past. He went away with his new friend and he never came back.

Roderigo went to the police to report him missing and a week later he was called to say that they'd found a body and would he come to identify it. The last time he saw his friend was through a window at the morgue. He'd been found stabbed in the back outside a big block of flats in the city, lying in the gutter. A day or two later a man in the building was arrested, who confessed to killing him for his watch and forty rand. Soon afterwards Roderigo left for Mozambique.

Why he tells this story I don't know, but there seems to be some kind of accusation in it. They finish their drinks in silence and go slowly back to the station. By now it's almost midday and the train is due to leave.

An hour or two into the journey they hear for the first time that Tanzania is about to hold its first multi-party elections in two days' time. The newspapers are full of stories of possible violence and upheaval, the rumours on the train are edged with nervousness. But none of this touches them, there is a new festive feeling amongst them all, as if they're going to a party.

But he lies awake that night for a long time after the others have drifted off, listening to the slow sound of breathing all around, the throbbing of the tracks. He worries about what he is going to do with himself when they leave in a few days, he will be alone in Tanzania in a politically unstable time, without a visa, with the prospect of retracing his route, step by step. Returning along the same path in any journey is depressing, but he especially fears how he might feel on this occasion.

The part of him that watches himself is still here too, not ecstatic or afraid. This part hovers in its usual detachment, looking down with wry amusement at the sleepless figure in the bunk. It sees all the complexities of the situation he's in and murmurs sardonically into his ear, you see where you have landed yourself. You intended to visit Zimbabwe for a few days and now you find yourself weeks later on a train to Dar es Salaam. Happy and unhappy, he falls asleep in the end and dreams about, no, I don't remember his dreams.

In the morning they are in a different landscape, out of the soft green hills and moving across a flat plain of bushveld. As they get closer to the coast they leave behind the yellow grass and thorn trees, now there is greenery outside again, the lush and verdant green of the tropics. The air is humid and hot, smelling of salt.

They arrive close to midday. There is no warning or announcement, the train simply comes to a stop at a siding and people get off. They can see the city a little distance away, clustered against the sky. They wonder where they might find a taxi, but a passing couple offers them a lift. The man is driving a new Range Rover and, while he negotiates the traffic, he tells them that he and his wife are both diplomats. He points to the little groups of people that are everywhere visible on the pavements, crouched down around radios on the ground, they are listening to reports on the elections, he says, there's been trouble in Zanzibar. What sort of trouble. Zanzibar voted two days ago, ahead of the rest of the country, now the results there have been announced but some of the parties have rejected them, there has been some fighting, some people throwing stones. And what about everywhere else, is there going to be trouble too. I don't think so, the man says, there's a lot of talk but nobody's going to do anything.

The couple drive them to a cheap hotel near the harbour. The place is almost full but they manage to get two rooms. Alice and Jerome and Christian are in one, Roderigo and I in the other. Everybody by now is becoming irritated by Roderigo, he is endlessly dissatisfied with everything and strident about announcing it. The prices of things are too high, the service is too poor, nothing measures up to his standards. Under his garish exterior he is endlessly fretful and unhappy. Now his anxiety is focused on the question of money. Back in Mbeya, it turns out, they discovered they have a problem. Aside from me, the others are all travelling with Visa cards, which no bank or business will accept here. It is ridiculous, Roderigo fumes, who has heard of such a thing, what a terrible and backward place this is.

On the train Christian has already approached me to borrow money, in Dar es Salaam he is sure they will be able to work something out. Now they all set off to try to find a place where they can draw money. He trails along in their wake, looking around at the city, while they go from one bank to another. But it's the same story, none of them accepts Visa cards. Some banks say that the card will not be usable anywhere and others tell them that certain banks will take it, just not this one. It's a long hot search. They have walked for blocks and are starting to feel dispirited and low when they are told to try one last place. This is up three flights of stairs in a narrow building close to their hotel. The bank is behind two massive wooden doors, outside which, in the dim stairwell, a guard lounges at a desk, wearing dark glasses. I'll wait here, he says, and sits down on the stairs. Christian and Alice and Roderigo go in through the wooden doors and suddenly he is left outside with Jerome.

This is the first time they've ever been alone together. Now that the moment is upon him so unexpectedly, he doesn't know what to do with it. He is sitting on the stairs, facing the guard, while Jerome moves up and down the darkened vestibule, looking uneasy. Then he turns and very quickly comes over to sit next to me on the step.

Only the speed at which he does this betrays how nervous he is. He takes hold of my arm in his hand.

With great difficulty, finding the words, he says, you want come in Switzerland with me.

I am astounded. Nothing has prepared the way for this question. My palms are sweating, my heart is hammering, but from the swirling behind my forehead only one question, the most stupid and irrelevant one possible, comes winding out, but what, I say, what will I do there.

You can work, he says.

Then the doors of the bank open, the others come out, he and Jerome pull away from each other, and they will never be alone again on this journey.

It's no good, Christian says. They won't take the card.

It's like being struck by lightning. Or like being pushed over an edge, on which, he now realizes, he's been balanced for days. Nothing is quite the same as before. When he follows the others down the stairs and out into the street he is looking at everything through a strange pane of glass, which both distorts and clarifies the world.

By now it's too late to go on searching, all the banks are closing for the day. But by now it's also clear that there's no solution to the problem. In the morning they will go to the French embassy, perhaps they will get help and advice there.

The rest of the day passes aimlessly, they go to the hotel next door to theirs to swim, they lie around, they talk. From

Jerome there is not the slightest trace of the strange feverishness that gripped him on the stairs. That night I go with them to the front desk of an expensive hotel nearby to phone. Alice and Jerome want to call their mother at home, it's been months since they spoke to her. It takes a long time to make the connection, they have to wait and wait in that vast echoey foyer. While he listens to this half of a conversation around the world, ah Maman, il est si bon d'entendre ta voix, the syllables of a language he doesn't understand convey an intimacy and affection that he does, and he can half-imagine this other life they come from, far to the north, which he's been invited to join. Should I go. Can I. His own life has narrowed to a fork, at which he dithers in an indecisive rapture.

He doesn't have to decide now, there is always tomorrow, tomorrow. But in the morning nothing has changed. He goes with them to the embassy to ask advice. We will lend you money, the people at the embassy say, go up to Kenya where you'll be able to use your card. There is a brief discussion but in fact there is no choice, without money there's nothing more they can do. They will go to Kenya the next morning. He knows already that they will ask him, they know already what he will say. Yes, I will come to Kenya with you.

I don't remember what they do the rest of that day. The next memory he has is of waking up in the middle of the night with the beam of a lighthouse flaring intermittently across the ceiling and the sound of Roderigo furtively masturbating under the sheets.

The next day is the election, but from the dusty windows of the bus the city looks the same as it did yesterday. It takes more than an hour to drive through the intricate alleys and little streets near the bus station. The complicated shop fronts with their myriad steps and tiny windows put him in mind of the innards of some enormous animal, through which they're creeping like a germ.

But once they're free of the city and on the open road the bus accelerates to alarming speed. They are being driven by a psychopathic Indian apparently bent on killing them all, overtaking on blind rises, racing some other bus to settle an old score, hurtling into corners without slowing down. A sort of dull terror comes down over him, he grips the seat and watches the outside world spill past like a dream. The road runs up in sight of the coast, across a broad green plain the flat water continually reappears, palm trees lagoons mangroves all the detritus of the tropics, little villages and settlements flash past, quick glimpses of other lives that glance off his in a tiny collision of images.

When they get to the border post he becomes anxious, what if they notice he has no visa. But he is out almost faster than the others, an exit stamp planted like a bruise next to the entry stamp he bought a few days ago. As they drive into Kenya it's dark already and a steady drizzle starts to fall. Nearing Mombasa, there are more and more people at the side of the road. The final approach is by ferry, on which they move across open water to the city, he stands outside at the rail and watches the yellow lights through the rain. The hotel they find is the most depressing one yet, two flights of stairs climb to their floor, the whole place seems made of untreated concrete, in the middle of each room a ceiling fan shudders and turns. The building doubles as a bordello, the floors underneath them are occupied by prostitutes who hang around in the foyer and on the pavement in front, hello my darling are you looking for me kssk kssk. They are in two rooms again, he and Roderigo apart from the rest, but a narrow balcony outside connects them. From this balcony there is a view across the street to a similar building facing them, in the different rooms of which they can see various sex acts in progress, each in its little lit cube.

This time the invitation doesn't come from Jerome, but from Alice. At lunch the next day there is a little moment of seriousness at the table, would you like to come with us, we have found a cheap flight to Athens, my mother has a house in a village in Greece. We are going there for a few weeks before we go home. He looks to Jerome, who says, come. But there is no echo of the last invitation on the stairs, this is a formal offer he could easily turn down.

And then, after Greece, he says. What will I do. Let me think, I will tell you later.

He goes walking through the old city, between high and fantastic facades, movement has always been a substitute for thought and he would like to stop thinking now. Wandering around, he finds himself in an antique shop full of cool dark air and oriental carpets and brass lamps, his eye slides off this material world until a human figure pulls it back. Where are you from. The man is in his fifties, white, with a big lined face and a lugubrious air. He has an improbable English accent, very overdone. South Africa, goodness me, how did you get up here. Through Malawi, my word, I'm off to Malawi in a few days. Look around, yes please, be my guest. What did you say your name was.

For some reason this lanky expat stays in his mind even when he gets back to the hotel, in all this grimy and half-decayed city he is the only other person, aside from his companions, who knows my name. He sits on the balcony as it gets dark, staring out into the hot rainy street, where a taxi pulls up and a prostitute gets out, one of the brightly dressed women from downstairs, along with a bearded white man his own age. They kiss lingeringly next to the car, their tongues flicker in the humid air, then the man gets back into the taxi and glides away.

When they all go out that night to eat, the mood around the table is glum. The others are weighed down by different thoughts, the end of nine months in Africa, maybe, the prospect of going home. But somewhere in the intermittent bits of conversation the question comes up again, have you decided what to do. No, not yet, in the morning.

That night he hardly sleeps. He throws himself around on the bed, he stares up at the fan as it turns and turns, he keeps getting up and wandering out onto the balcony and then wandering back again. His brain is boiling over, he can't make it cool down.

In the morning everybody is up early. There is a lot of commotion and activity, and it's a while before Jerome comes in to ask with raised eyebrows, good decision.

He shakes his head, his voice won't come out properly. I must go back.

Jerome doesn't answer, but his face goes tight.

So the journey ends with four little words. Nobody argues with him, they are all caught up with what they have to do, sorting through their things and packing their bags. He doesn't want to sit around watching, so he tells Christian he's going out for a walk.

We must go by ten.

I'll be back by then.

He goes out through the crowded streets, he wanders without any plan clear to himself, but he's not surprised when he finds himself back at the dark antique shop. The seedy expat is there again, balanced with a cup of coffee on a pile of carpets. I was here yesterday, I tell him.

Oh yes, he says vaguely.

You mentioned you were going to Malawi in a few days.

Yes. Yes. I am thinking of doing that.

I wondered whether you might want a companion on the trip.

At this the dark eyes lighten a little, oh yes, he says, that would be good. Why don't you come by tomorrow and we can make plans. What is your name again.

Damon. My name is Damon.

The man repeats his name. He goes back to the hotel by half past nine, but there's no sign of the others. At first he assumes they're out somewhere having breakfast, but then it dawns on him that they've gone, when Christian said ten he must've meant the time at which the bus actually left, they are at the bus-station by now.

He thinks he must hurry over to say goodbye. But by the time he's downstairs again another conviction comes slowly over him. Isn't it better this way, let them go quietly without seeing them. So he starts to wander through the streets again, but in the wrong direction, away from the bus-station, looking at people, at shops, at any detail he passes that might distract his mind. He can already feel the next few days stretching away in these aimless and awful walks of his, there is nothing more sordid than having to use up time.

But then suddenly he is off, running the other way through the crowds. Where does this movement come from, it takes even him by surprise, he is looking for a taxi but none appears out of the dense traffic. He arrives at the bus-station with only minutes to spare and then he has to look for the bus. When he finds it the engine is already running, a man at the door tells him there's still space. Go in, get a seat, I give you a ticket now. No, no, I want to say goodbye to my friends.

They all get off, assembling at the edge of the road with a dejected air, none of them quite looking at each other. He would like to say something, the perfect single word that contains how he feels, but there isn't any such word. Instead he says nothing, he makes half gestures that die before he can complete them, he shakes his head and sighs.

Goodbye, he says.

You will come in Switzerland, yes, Jerome says again.

All of this is spoken flatly, there is no trace of feeling in the whole little scene, and by now the driver is hooting impatiently at them. We have to go, Christian says. Yes, I say, goodbye. I lean forward and grip Jerome by the upper arm and squeeze hard. I promise you I will see you again.

Goodbye.

He and Alice smile at each other, then she turns and goes up the steps. Roderigo reaches out to embrace him, my friend take care of yourself, the odd one out is the most effusive of all.

He walks slowly back through the racket and chaos. It hasn't dawned on him yet what's happened. When he gets back to the hotel he pays the proprietor downstairs for another night, and while he's fumbling through his wallet for change he feels a furtive hand tugging at his fly. He jumps back in fright, the hand belongs to one of the prostitutes, perhaps the same one he saw kissing in the street last night, her vivid lips smile at him in the gloom. I'm just trying to help you, she says.

I don't need help.

The vehemence of his tone is startling, she makes an ooing noise to mock him, he breaks away and goes up the stairs. Somehow this incident has set his feelings free, a thin column of grief rises in him like mercury. He goes into his room and stares around, then goes out along the balcony to their room. It's all as it was, the three beds, the fan turning listlessly over-head. He sits down on the edge of a chair. There are bits of paper crumpled on the floor, envelopes, notes, pages from a book, which they dropped while cleaning out their bags, and these solitary white scraps, drifting in the wind from the fan, are sadder to him than anything else that's happened.

Jerome, if I can't make you live in words, if you are only the dim evocation of a face under a fringe of hair, and the others too, Alice and Christian and Roderigo, if you are names without a nature, it's not because I don't remember, no, the opposite is true, you are remembered in me as an endless stirring and turning. But it's for this precisely that you must forgive me, because in every story of obsession there is only one character, only one plot. I am writing about myself alone, it's all I know, and for this reason I have always failed in every love, which is to say at the very heart of my life.

He sits in the empty room, crying.

H e's not prepared for how bad the next few days turn out to be. He spends a lot of time lying on his back on the bed, staring up at the fan on the ceiling. Then he suddenly can't take it any more and jumps up and goes out into the streets, striding along as if he has a purpose and a destination, but these walks always peter out at some point, often in an alley at the edge of the sea, where he stares into the haze, at a dhow going past.

He goes back to the antique shop a couple of times. The expat, whose name is Charles, is always vague about his plans, but he insists that, yes, he will be going to Malawi. He just wants to wait a day or two, he says, till this election thing is over in Tanzania, you can never be sure, you know, this is Africa after all. In these conversations he always has to ask my name at some point, before immediately forgetting it again.

Meanwhile he prepares for his return, he goes to the consulate and gets a proper visa for Tanzania. Then he goes to the health office down at the harbour to get the vaccinations he needs. The Indian doctor he speaks to tells him smilingly how much they will cost, then leans forward confidentially and says, do you actually want these vaccinations.

I don't understand.

You can pay and have the vaccinations, or you can pay and not have the vaccinations, I don't mind, it's up to you.

He pays and doesn't have the vaccinations, he is learning the way things work. As long as the stamp on the paper is correct, what the stamp is supposed to signify doesn't matter to anyone.

The third time he goes back, Charles is more animated than usual. We can leave the day after tomorrow, he says, how does that suit you. The results of the Tanzanian election have come out, but the whole process has been denounced as highly irregular, it has to be started again from the beginning. It doesn't look like there's going to be trouble, Charles says, they're behaving themselves. There is only one thing, I stay out of town, come and spend the day there tomorrow.

He is there in the morning and they drive out soon after in Charles's battered van. They go back on the ferry and along the road to the coast. He spends his last day in Kenya at a resort on the beach near to where Charles lives with his family.

This is also the day on which the others are leaving Kenya, he knows the time of their flight. So at two that afternoon, while he stands on a deserted beach of glimmering white sand, gazing out into an ocean that stretches in gradations of deepening colour towards a line of surf that marks the reef far out, he looks at his watch and feels their departure almost as a physical change in himself. His heart missing a beat, say. You are going down the runway, you are lifting into the air, you are banking slowly to the north and moving away, away.

It's about now that he realizes he has made a mistake. He should have gone with them, of course he should. Why is he going home. It's only a couple of days later, but already his decision is senseless. He sees clearly what he's going back to in South Africa, the same state of nothing, the drifting from place to place. Never has this condition so obviously been what it is, an absence of love. He feels sick with the meaning of what he's done.

But it isn't too late. What rises in him now is an urge to make the largest and most dramatic gesture of all, he will chase them not for a few hundred kilometres but halfway across the world. He spends the afternoon walking up and down the beach, crossing and recrossing his own tracks between the palm trees, while he works out what to do. It's entirely possible. He must get back down to South Africa as quickly as he can, he must scrape some money together, he must fly to Greece in a few days. On the piece of paper from the Tanzanian border he has Jerome's home number, where his mother is. He must phone her and find out where they are, how to get to this holiday house. He will make his way there from Athens, he will arrive one night out of the dark, out of the recent past, with his hands open, smiling. It's me again, I came here to find you.

He's still knotted up when he and Charles set off the next morning. Charles is wearing shorts and sandals and a big straw hat on his head. He is a good-looking man in a loose, bigboned sort of way, but if you study him closely begin to see the signs of decay. His nails are dirty, he has nicotine stains on his teeth, around his eyes the lines are as deep and dark as old bruises. There is something in his spirit that resembles an overripe fruit, soft and pulpy at the centre. Just before they get to the border he pulls over in a cane-field and lights up a huge joint. To calm me down, he says, before I deal with these bastards.

It turns out he's smuggling twenty thousand dollars' worth of Afghan rugs under two oil drums in the back. These are destined, he tells me afterwards, for one or another official at the American embassy in Dar es Salaam, they are one of the reasons he's making this trip. Charles sweats and trembles like a junkie as they go across the border, but afterwards he affects a bored composure. No problem if they were found, he says breezily, a quick fifty dollars and they'll look the other way. I know these chaps, I speak the lingo.

When they arrive at Dar es Salaam in the evening he takes them to a vast house in one of the more exclusive suburbs, with a metal fence and a security guard outside. It's the residence of some highup official in the embassy, a plump middle-aged woman with glasses who comes out to meet them, smiling broadly.

She agrees to let them stay over, and he finds himself in a luxurious bedroom, drapes and thick carpets and a bathroom tiled to the ceiling. It's unreal to him, but not as unreal as dinner that night, which they have with the Romanian ambassador to Tanzania. For some bizarre reason there is a portrait of Lenin on the wall and the ambassador makes a sign of the cross in self-defence when he sees it. I am silent under the weight of this surreal situation, and glad to be alone in bed not long after. In the passage outside the door a radio crackles and burps all night, leaking American voices talking in code.

The next day they drive to Mbeya and put up in a hotel. Since leaving Kenya Charles hasn't called me anything, but that night, in the bar, I hear him saying, Noel, Noel, and when I look around Charles is speaking to me. Why he's fixed on this name it's hard to tell, but I feel too weary to correct him. By this time there is a high level of irritation between them and being called Noel is just part of the deal.

By the next day, when they enter Malawi, the irritation is teetering on the edge of argument. When they miss a turning somewhere Charles starts to berate him, you're supposed to be watching the road signs, Noel, and he has to force himself to stay silent. Later Charles expatiates on what lies beneath the Malawians' smiles, they're pretending to be innocent but they're a crafty lot, I've seen this before. Don't be fooled, Noel, I've got their number.

It's time to move on and the next morning, when they get to the lake, he says goodbye. Charles is alarmed, why don't you hang around for a while, he doesn't want to be left alone with the crafty Malawians. But the South African shakes his head, in two days he can be back at home, his mind wanders constantly northward, to Greece. Oh all right, Charles mutters defeatedly, go then. But write your address in my book, in case I ever come to Cape Town.

I hesitate with the book in hand, not knowing what to write. But after a moment I print my new name, Noel, and an old telephone number, I will never hear from Charles again.

From here the return journey goes swiftly, Noel jumps from one bus to another, only pausing to overnight in Blantyre. In another two days he is back in South Africa, in Pretoria. It has taken him six days to get back from Mombasa, half the length of the continent.

The whole way home he has thought of nothing but what it is he wants to do, he has been consumed by the desire to get to Greece. But now something happens to him. Back among familiar things again, the objects and faces that are the icons of his usual life, a kind of apathy comes over him. It's as if he's in shock. Did I really do that, he thinks to himself, did I really go chasing them all that way. And instead of rushing out in a continuation of his old momentum to book tickets and make plans, he finds himself sitting in the sun, brooding about what's happened. He feels even less sure than before about the meaning of it all.

By imperceptible degrees, then, he accepts the notion that the journey is over, and that he's back where he started. The story of Jerome is one he's lived through before, it is the story of what never happened, the story of travelling a long way while standing still.

In dreams he is constantly looking at maps, in which there are continents and countries, but they don't resemble the actual world. In these maps real countries are joined together in peculiar new configurations, Mexico at the top of Africa, next to Borneo. Or else countries have mythical names and shapes which evoke a longing in him. He has always been drawn by the strangeness of places, by what he doesn't know instead of what he does.

Four months later he goes to Europe. Spring has only just started and the streets of Amsterdam are cold as he walks and walks. He takes a bus to Brussels, he goes by train to Strasbourg. He visits a friend in the Black Forest for a while and then, on a bright morning with the first trace of warmth in the air, he takes a train south, to Switzerland.

He has written to say he's coming and from Germany, a few days before, he made a call. Jerome was not at home and when Alice came to the phone she sounded startled but happy. Yes, she said, please come to visit, we are waiting for you. But now, as the train slides and turns through the mountains, emerging at last into the bright open sky over the lake, he has a faint memory again of the fear that gripped him in Africa. He stands at the window, looking at the houses and little streets flashing past at the edge of the water, and feels doubt like a coldness in him.

He has to change trains and take a smaller local line along the lake. He climbs out on the fifth or sixth stop and descends the stairs into a stone square, from which narrow streets slope down towards the water. The lake is silvery-grey in colour, with hardly a crease on its surface, and on the other side, far away, mountains rise to sharp and jagged crests.

Now that he has waited so long and come so far, he is in no hurry to arrive. He sits on the shore for a long time, thinking. He would like this moment to suspend itself indefinitely, so that he need never stir himself again.

But as the afternoon goes on he takes up his pack and walks back along the lake, in the direction from which the train came. The path narrows and goes under trees, past jetties. There are swans gliding in the water, supported on their own reflections. After half an hour he comes to a little street running up away from the lake, and its name is the one written on that scrap of paper from Malawi.

The house is a largish one, set back from the corner, with a garden behind it. He knocks and after a while there are footsteps and the door opens. Hello, we have been waiting for you.

Jerome's mother has short hair and a wide welcoming smile, come in, come in. She seems genuinely pleased to see him, she holds out her hand. My name is Catherine.

While they shake hands they look appraisingly at each other. He has no idea what she has been told about him or what she expects. Jerome has just come home, she tells him, it is a surprise. He was supposed to come only tomorrow. He will be so glad to see you. She calls to a young girl hovering nearby, go and find Jerome.

While they wait they go to sit on a stone veranda behind the house. In the garden there is a tree, a swing, and through a screen of leaves at the bottom, a view of the water. Alice comes out, smiling. There is the awkward happiness of hello, hello, how are you, looking at each other while they also look away.

When Jerome comes out he is wearing a blue military uniform and his hair is cut brutally short. They shake hands, smiling shyly, under the eyes of his mother and Alice. Ah hello yes excellent. Jerome, I'm glad to see you. The dialogue and the gestures are tinny and false, like some kind of bright paper wrapped around the meaning of the moment.

They all settle down uneasily around the outdoor table. The girl who was sent off to find Jerome is his younger sister. She is fourteen or fifteen with a chubby, cheerful face. An older sister arrives soon afterwards. Conversation flickers back and forth, returning continually to him, he can sense how curious they are about him. But at the same time he is also an observer, watching Jerome in this circle of women, while the light fades away.

Why don't you go for a walk, Catherine says. Before supper.

He goes with Jerome across the grass to a gate at the bottom of the garden. Through a narrow alley to the edge of the lake. They are alone again for the first time since that minute or two outside the wooden doors of the bank. But everything is different now. The artificial awkwardness of that first moment up at the house continues, they don't know what to say to each other.

So this is where you live.

Yes. Yes.

It's beautiful here.

Ah. Yes. I like.

Only once does the mask of tension crack briefly, when I ask him, is it hard to be back.

Yes. Yes. His mouth works to find the words. In my head I am travelling, travelling.

I know what you mean.

Jerome is doing a session of military service, he is only home for the weekend. While he's here they share his room, the visitor sleeps on a mattress on the floor. Although this section of the house is apart from the rest, a separate little flat on its own, they are never away from the rest of the family. It's pleasant to sit in the sun behind the house, talking with Catherine, or wander to the shops with Alice or one of the other sisters. Jerome is always kind and solicitous, he invites him wherever he goes and introduces him to his friends, and he lets himself be taken along on outings and play the part of a contented guest.

On the Sunday Jerome's father comes to visit. He has lived apart from them, at the other end of the lake, for some years now, and in the family his departure has left the lingering trace of a loss. So on this day, when they make a fire to cook in the yard, and knock a ball back and forth over a net, there is a feeling of completion and unity among them, to which I can only be a witness. He sits on the swing, pushing himself to and fro, watching as if from a great distance this scene that in Africa would be unimaginable to him.

He has come to like all of them, so when Jerome leaves again that night, going by train to some military base at the other end of the country, he is not alarmed at being left with his family. He spends a lot of time walking along the lake, he takes the train into town and wanders there too. He spends a day in a gallery of outsider art, paintings and sculptures made with the vision of the mad or the lost, and from this collection of fantastic and febrile images he retains a single line, a book title by a Serbian artist whose name I forget, He Has No House.

On the next weekend Jerome is back again, but if he was hoping that the gap of five days would change something between them, it doesn't happen. They are pleasant and polite with each other, but their interaction has something of the quality of a letter which Jerome sent him, the studied and careful presentation of words that have been translated and copied from a dictionary. It isn't only Jerome who makes things this way, he brings his own painful awkwardness to bear. He isn't himself, he is a guarded version of his own nature, nor does he recognize in the cropped hair and military terseness of the person whose room he shares the soft and gentle young man he travelled with four months ago.

There are hints, perhaps, that it might be possible to move past this state. Jerome makes some tentative conversation about plans he has for the future, how, when he's finished with this stint in the army, he would like to travel overland down to Greece. But this will only be in a couple of months from now. The possibility of another shared journey floats in the air, both of them consider it, but neither of them has the courage to say anything more.

He knows already that he must move on. On the night before Jerome gets back that next weekend, he takes a walk along the water. Mist is rolling in from the other side, smudging the outlines of the little boats at their moorings. When he comes to a jetty that projects a long way into the lake he walks out on the wooden planks to the end. From here there is no shore any more, no edge to anything he can see. He is adrift in the white mist, with the water slapping softly below, cold air rolling across his face. He leans on the railing and stares into the whiteness and thinks about everything that's happened.

When Jerome returns this time, he finds a moment to let him know, I will be going on Monday. To London. I can't stay here for ever. I'm sure your family must be getting tired of me.

No, no. Jerome is vehement in his protest. You can stay.

He shakes his head gently and smiles, I have to go, I can't keep standing still.

Later Jerome comes back to him again, bringing a friend who lives a few houses away. This friend speaks fluent English and has come along, he says, to translate.

Jerome says you must stay.

No, really. Tell him thank you. But I can't. Maybe I will come back.

When, Jerome says.

Later. When I've gone travelling for a while.

And it's true, he tells himself, maybe he will come back. There is always another time, next month, next year, when things will be different.

But after these flickers of feeling, that last weekend is much like the others. Jerome is friendly but distant, he makes no special effort to talk or be alone. At one point he says, we talk with Christian, yes, and picks up the phone. But the number just rings and rings. Jerome says, later, and puts it down again, but they never do try later.

On the Sunday evening when Alice drives her brother to the station, he goes along to say goodbye. Jerome is in uniform again, with all his buttons gleaming, his black shoes reflecting the light. He is proud of how he looks, although he pretends that he isn't. They all go into the bar together to wait. There are two friends of his there, also in uniform, with whom he'll be travelling, there are introductions and handshakes and murmured pleasantries all round.

You go tomorrow, Jerome says at last.

Yes.

But you come again later.

Maybe.

One of the friends says something and all of them stand up. Sorry. We must to go.

In the end they shake hands again, smiling formally, amongst all the artificial surfaces and military buttons shining like eyes. They have never been more distant, or polite. In the morning his actual departure will be an echo of this one. He has already left, or perhaps he never arrived.

He goes to London, but the same restlessness comes over him there, and he goes on somewhere else. And somewhere else again. Five months later he finds himself in a strange country, at the edge of a strange town, with dusk coming down. He is watching people drifting into a funfair on the other side of an overgrown expanse of ground. Circus music carries towards him faintly over the weeds and in the gathering gloom at the base of a high green volcano he sees the lights of a ferris wheel go round and round and round.

He doesn't know why, but this scene is like a mirror in which he sees himself. Not his face, or his past, but who he is. He feels a melancholy as soft and colourless as wind, and for the first time since he started travelling he thinks that he would like to stop. Stay in one place, never move again.

Eight months after he passed through he is in London again, on his way back home. He is only here for a week, after which he will fly to Amsterdam and then, five days later, to South Africa.

He phones Jerome from a booth in the street. He doesn't know exactly why he's making this call, except that he promised he would, and he's unsure of whether to go back to visit them again. Before he can even mention the idea Jerome has put it to him, come, come, please. This time, even through the thin vein of the telephone line, he can hear the urgency of the invitation.

I have to think, he says, I have no money.

My family, it's okay, no money.

Also no time. I have only four days before I go. Maybe, all right, I'll see. I'll phone you from Amsterdam.

But before he gets to Amsterdam he has already made up his mind not to go. It's true that he has little money and time, but these are not the reasons for his decision. The memory of the last visit is still strong in his mind, he has carried it with him all the way on his travels, and he fears that the same thing will happen again. He will arrive, he will be made very welcome, he will spend a day or two in placidity and comfort, but the silence and distance between them, which they have incubated somehow since the first day they met in Africa, will amplify and grow, even as they become nicer to each other. This isn't what he wants, it is very deeply what he doesn't want, although it has taken this short conversation on the telephone for him to realize how unhappy that first visit made him.

So he goes down to Paris instead and stumbles aimlessly around the streets, wandering into shops and out again, sitting on benches. He's aware that he's engaged again in that most squalid of activities, using up time, but the journey hasn't ended where he wanted it to, it has frayed out instead into endless ambiguities and nuances, like a path that divides and divides endlessly, growing fainter all the time.

There are moments, it's true, in those three or four days, when a longing to go back to Switzerland comes over him like a pang, it's only a few hours on the train, he could do it on a whim, but then he remembers how he came back this way last time, emptiness weighing him down like a black suitcase chained to his wrist.

When he passes a public telephone now and then he remembers that he promised to call, but he can't do it yet, not yet. There would be a discussion again on the line, the push and pull of their broken attempts to communicate, and he might give in, in spite of himself.

So he leaves it to what is the very last moment, when he is at the airport in Amsterdam, with his bag checked in, waiting to board. There are crowds of people under the fluorescent lights, clutching packets from the duty-free shops, and outside, through the plateglass windows, the weird unnatural shapes of aircraft in rows. He makes the call from a bank of public phones, jostled from either side by elbows and foreign syllables. He hopes that Jerome won't be home.

Catherine answers the phone and recognizes his voice before he's said his name. Hello, are you coming back to visit us.

No, I'm sorry, I can't. I'm at the airport right now.

Ahh. She sounds disappointed. What a pity, we were hoping, Jerome was hoping.

I know, I'm sorry about it. He starts to babble the excuses about money and time, but his tongue is tripping him up. Another time, he says, and now he means it, there will be another time to make this right.

Another time, she agrees, do you want to talk to Jerome, and though his money is fast running out he knows he must.

There is a brief conversation in the background before Jerome comes on, in his voice he knows already. Ah, but why.

No money, he says again, no time.

Come. Come.

It's too late. I'm at the airport. I'll make it up to you, he says, I promise. Another time.

Yes, I want. Travelling. Next year.

Where.

I don't know. Africa. Possibly.

That will be wonderful, he says. It sounds as if he's been invited, although the words, as always, haven't been said. Jerome, I have to go. The money.

I don't understand.

And then the phone goes dead. He hangs up slowly, wondering whether to ring again, but he's said what he has to say, and anyway he has to leave. Another time.

Friends who live in London have bought a house in the country three hours from Cape Town, and when I was passing through they offered the use of this place to stay in. If you think you would like it, it's going to be standing empty, it would be nice to have somebody keeping an eye.

He said he would think about it but the next day, just before leaving London, he phoned to accept. It felt in some way like a providential offer. He has no other place to return to, and he knows he can't go back to the way he was living before, the endless moving around, the rootlessness. So the idea of this house, far away from all the old familiar sites, is like a fresh beginning, the possibility of home.

The move isn't easy, he has to take all his things out of storage and hire vans to load everything up and conscript friends to help him drive. The house, when he gets there, is like nowhere he's ever lived before. It's rustic and rough, with a thatched roof and concrete floors and a windmill turning outside the bedroom window. His friends help him unload and then drive back to Cape Town almost immediately, leaving him alone amongst the piles and piles of boxes.

That first night he sits on the back step, looking out across a back yard choked with weeds to the occasional lights of trucks on the single road that passes the town. He watches the moon come up over the stony tops of the valley and gets gently drunk on sherry and wonders what he's done to himself now.

But over the next few days, as he sweeps and cleans and unpacks the boxes and puts his possessions into place, he starts to feel better about where he is. It doesn't belong to him, but he lives here, he doesn't need to leave unless he wants to. And as the shapes of the rooms and the noises of the roof become familiar, a sort of intimacy develops between him and the place, they put out tendrils and grow into each other. This process deepens as his life overflows outdoors, he starts pulling up the weeds in the garden, he digs furrows and lets water run to the fruit trees and the rose-bushes, and when old dead branches begin to sprout buds and leaves, and then bright bursts of colour, he feels as if it's happening inside himself.

By then the little town and even the landscape around it are also connected to him, there is no interruption between him and the world, he isn't separate any more from what he sees. When he goes out the front door now it isn't to catch a bus, or to find another hotel, he walks into the mountains and then he comes back home again. Home. Sometimes he stops on whatever dirt road he's followed today and looks back down the valley to the town, and then he always picks out the tiny roof under which he will be sleeping tonight.

He doesn't feel like a traveller any more, it's hard to imagine that he ever thought of himself that way, and when he finally settles himself to write a letter to Jerome it's like a stranger willing up the words. He tells about where he is and what it's like to be here, and says that he hopes Jerome will come to visit him one day.

A week after he sends the letter an envelope arrives from Switzerland. He doesn't recognize the handwriting, but the stamp is clearly visible, and it's with a sense of excitement that he sits down to read. When he opens the envelope his own letter falls out, like a piece of the past returned to his hands. The single stiff card that accompanies it says, Dear Sir, I'm very sorry to break the death of Jerome to you. He died on the 26th of November in an accident of motorbike. His mother asked me to send you your letter back. The signature at the bottom is that of a stranger, and even as he sits at the epicentre of this soundless white explosion, that separate watchful part of his brain is back again, reading over his shoulder, trying to decipher the name, aware of all the oddities of language, working out when it happened. One week to the day after I got back home.

A journey is a gesture inscribed in space, it vanishes even as it's made. You go from one place to another place, and on to somewhere else again, and already behind you there is no trace that you were ever there. The roads you went down yesterday are full of different people now, none of them knows who you are. In the room you slept in last night a stranger lies in the bed. Dust covers over your footprints, the marks of your fingers are wiped off the door, from the floor and table the bits and pieces of evidence that you might have dropped are swept up and thrown away and they never come back again. The very air closes behind you like water and soon your presence, which felt so weighty and permanent, has completely gone. Things happen once only and are never repeated, never return. Except in memory.

He sits for a long time at the table, not seeing, not hearing anything. When he feels strong enough to move he gets up very slowly and locks the house and goes out, walking into the world. His body feels old and through the dark lens on his eyes everything he knows looks strange and unfamiliar, as if he's lost in a country he's never visited before.

THREE

THE GUARDIAN

E ven before their departure, when he goes to meet her flight from Cape Town, he knows he's in trouble. He last saw her a month ago and she was in a bad way then, but look at her now. The first one off the plane, striding far ahead of the crowd. Her peroxide job has gone wrong, so that her hair has turned a strange yellow colour, standing out in angry spikes from her head. But more than this, something has changed inside her, which you can see from a long way off. She seems to burn with a luminous white light. Her face is knotted and anxious, bunched in on itself, and it takes her a long time to notice him. Then her expression clears, she smiles, as they embrace she is his old friend again.

He has been up in Pretoria for a few weeks, visiting his mother. But even before he left Cape Town, Anna was already losing the plot, living in fast motion, speeding along, saying and doing inappropriate things, and the knowledge that she was out of control showed in her face like a concealed pain. All of this has happened before, but it's only a few days ago that her condition has finally acquired a name. Although it's come from her psychiatrist in Cape Town, the diagnosis is one which Anna's lover and I and even Anna herself all regard with suspicion. For us she remains human first and foremost, impervious to labels.

He is pretty sure about all this until he sees her. It's obvious that something in her has come loose from its moorings and is sliding around inside. There are problems ahead, I realize, and the first moment comes before we've even left the ground. In the departure lounge she orders a beer, then looks at her companion in bemusement as he stares.

What. What's the matter.

You're not supposed to be doing that. We spoke about this yesterday, remember.

It's just one drink.

You're not allowed even one drink.

She has come with a small pharmacy in her bag, tranquillizers and mood-stabilizers and anti-depressants, which have to be taken in various combinations at different times, but alcohol or recreational drugs will undo the medication, and she solemnly swore to me over the telephone the day before that she wouldn't touch them. She has given the same pledge to both her lover and her psychiatrist.

When I remind her of this promise she angrily cancels the order, but no sooner has the plane taken off than she orders a double whisky. A little drink every now and then, she says, won't do me any harm. I'm speechless at her defiance, but the incident is rapidly subsumed in an ongoing disorder. When the food arrives she messes it over herself, then clambers over another passenger on her way to the bathroom to clean up. As the journey goes on, she becomes frantic to the point of tears because she's not allowed to smoke a cigarette, and when they arrive in Bombay after midnight she spends the long taxi ride into town unzipping and rummaging through all the pockets of her rucksack in search of some missing item. Once they're installed at the hotel she becomes a bit calmer, but almost immediately she leaves him in the room, locking the door behind her, and goes to the rooftop restaurant for yet another little drink.

On the last occasion that she went off the rails, years ago, she landed in a Cape Town clinic, emaciated and scarred with cigarette burns. It took months for her to recover, a process that she fetishized in her photographs, many of them pictures of herself naked, all her wounds on display. The episode is sexy in her mind, no cause for shame, and culminated in several bouts of electro-shock therapy, which she'd asked for, she later told me, as a substitute for killing herself.

It's partly to avoid a repetition of the same scenario that he's invited her to come along with him on this, his third trip to India. He's going for six months and the plan is that Anna will join him for the first eight weeks. And it seemed in the beginning like a good idea to everybody. Back home in Cape Town she has a powerful job with a very high profile and a future full of impressive possibilities. Normally she is more than a match for the challenges of her work, attacking it with a fervour that now looks suspect. But both her job and her relationship are under strain at the moment, and this is meant to be time out. A couple of months away from home, a chance for Anna to find herself and stabilize. Maybe it's just what she needs.

Although the start has been tough, things will be easier, he reasons, when they reach their destination. They are heading for a tiny fishing village in south Goa, where he has spent the previous two winters. There will be nothing to do except lie around in the sun or go for long walks on the beach or swim in the warm sea. Surely the indolence will slow her down. Besides, as her psychiatrist has said, it will take a couple of weeks for the medicine to kick in properly. Better times lie ahead.

Before they can fully relax, however, there is still one more journey to get through, and on the train the next day a new drama develops. He is strict about supervising her medication, and even in the rocking train carriage he makes sure that she counts out her assortment of pills. As she starts swallowing them he turns away, but sees from the corner of one eye the jerk of her arm as she throws a tablet out of the window. What are you doing. She instantly breaks down weeping, I can't handle it, these tranquillizers knock me out, I can't function. He feels a stab of pity, at this early point he still has patience and compassion. You have to take them, Anna, your body will adjust.

He will soon establish, when he sits down to examine the note from her psychiatrist, that she's been double-dosing on one of the tranquillizers, and when this imbalance has been corrected the medicine won't touch her. But right now she sleeps most of the journey away, while he stares out of the window at the changing landscape outside. He is glad of this chance just to reflect quietly, while the dry vastness of the plains gives way by degrees to the lush, steamy heat of Goa.

He is middle-aged now and his travelling habits have changed. He has become more sedentary, staying in one place for longer periods of time, with less of that youthful rushing around. But this new approach has its problems. On a previous trip to India, waiting in a town far to the north for some bureaucratic business to be finished, he became aware that he was forming connections with the place, giving money to a sick man here, calling the vet to attend to a stray dog there, setting up a web of habits and social reflexes that he usually travels to escape. He wonders now if he hasn't taken a step further down that road by bringing his troubled friend with him on the trip. Here they are, barely arrived, and already he feels chords of alarm twanging deep down. But the motion and heat are numbing, and he's calmer by the time evening comes and they have broken out at last into paddy fields and stretches of blue water between palm trees. Anna wakes and looks out of the window in amazement. Are we there yet. Almost.

The sun is setting as they reach Margao, a dirty bustling town like countless others they've passed along the way, but fortunately there's no need for them to linger. Their destination is a twenty minute ride by auto-rickshaw through tracts of greenery with the last golden light cooling overhead, and somewhere along the way she puts a hand on his arm and tells him how beautiful it is. Thank you for bringing me, she says. I'm so glad to be here.

When they arrive at the little family-run hotel where he usually stays, there are familiar faces to welcome them and a room has been kept aside. He takes a shower and when he comes downstairs to the restaurant she's drinking a gin-and-tonic. Oh come on, she cries when she sees his face, I'm on holiday, what do you want from me.

He and Anna have a good friendship, she is like a sister to him, somebody he loves and who makes him laugh. Somebody he wants to protect. It's in that capacity that he's escorting her now, as her guardian. In that last telephone conversation before she left Cape Town, the same one in which she promised never to drink, she had asked him, almost as a challenge, are you up to it, do you think you can handle me. He'd answered breezily, not thinking about it much, yes of course. It didn't feel like a heavy undertaking at the time, because he's always had a cooling, calming influence on her, she's always listened to him. But already, just a few days into the trip, he understands that they're playing by a new set of rules. She and he have always been on the same side, but it's as if she's changed allegiances somehow, to who or what he doesn't know, though he comes gradually to understand that the danger to Anna, the force from which she must be protected, is inside her.

He gets an inkling of how strong that force is when, out of curiosity, he takes half of one of her tranquillizers. The effect is devastating. He's wiped out, flat on his back, for twelve hours, and for the whole of the next day he's groggy and weak. After that he looks at her with a new awareness. She's swallowing these pills three times a day and they don't appear even to slow her down any more. What is this thing that's taken up station inside her, driving along with so much fury and power.

Her illness, which he comes to think of as a person separate to Anna, makes her behave in bizarre and unsettling ways. The drinking is one sign, but there are others. She has an obsession with packing and unpacking her rucksack, at any time of the day or night this compulsion overcomes her, then there is the manic flurrying of zips, the clothing piled up on the bed. He watches with troubled fascination as she separates different items into different compartments, shirts here, panties there, dresses somewhere else again, and each set of garments is packed into a plastic bag with a label on it. When he points out to her how crazy this is she laughs and agrees with him, but it doesn't stop her from repeating the exercise just a couple of hours later. And she's awake every morning at first light. She has been given sleeping pills, which she's supposed to take every night, but often she doesn't bother, then he is awoken by the noise of her blundering and fumbling as she goes out onto the balcony for her first cigarette, sorry did I disturb you, I was trying to be quiet. Nor do the other pills appear to be working. Her moods continue to veer wildly between elation and despair, she can be laughing at breakfast and sobbing by mid-morning, he doesn't know how to cope with these extremes.

Nevertheless, they manage to have a good time together. The beach is just down the road and they spend hours there each day. They walk and swim and Anna takes hundreds of photographs, clicking the shutter voraciously, sucking the world into her camera in rectangular pieces, the fishing boats on the sea, the sun rising and setting, drops of water on dark skin, the faces of people passing by. When I look at these images now, years later, they call back a sense of idyll and inno-cence which perhaps was never true, not even then. Though I know from other visits how fine a place it is, and if the air is disturbed every now and then by the death-screams of a pig, well, there is slaughter even in paradise.

I t's on one of the first evenings, as they sit on their balcony together, that she says, it would be so nice if we could make love. He looks at her in astonishment. She quickly adds, I know it's impossible, but I was just thinking.

A long silence follows. Their room is on the first floor, on a level with the tops of the palm trees in the yard, and in the last light the fronds take on a soft, reflected glow. Anna, he says. We can't.

I know, I know, forget it.

Your girlfriend is my best friend. And I don't think about you in that way.

I shouldn't have said it.

Anyway, I thought you weren't into men.

She giggles. You know, she says, I'm not so sure. I've been having some thoughts.

This is something new. He knows that she was seriously involved with one or two men quite long ago, but in recent years she's been adamantly inclined in the other direction. He wonders whether it's not just a reaction to the strain her relationship is under at home. Anna hasn't once written to her partner back in Cape Town, she hasn't made a single phone call, and when I've encouraged her to get in touch she only shakes her head. She doesn't want to, she says, she thinks it's over between them, but he knows that her partner has been hurt by Anna's silence.

He doesn't push the point, it's not his business, and anyway he thinks she'll feel differently in a few days. But he experiences a complicated guilt when, perhaps that very same night, or perhaps another soon after, she goes with some American man to his room. We didn't make love, she tells me afterwards, we just fooled around, but oh it was so wonderful to be held, to be touched like that.

This puts him into a horrible position, where his loyalties are divided. He's in regular contact with Anna's girlfriend back home, reporting on her condition, but how can he talk about this. Yet Anna is counting on his silence, she would regard it as betrayal if he spilled the beans. He's angry that she's made him complicit in what may be a widening gap, so it comes as a relief when the American takes fright. The next night, when she tries to arrange a liaison, he tells her that he has some important e-mails to write, and the following day he leaves town.

But she doesn't give up. The idea is in her head now and she's on the search. She's a strikingly pretty woman and in her current state especially so, lean and glowing with inner fire. All kinds of men are sniffing around. In just a day or two she meets Jean, a fifty year old French traveller staying at the same hotel. When I come to the room that night after doing e-mail I find the two of them sitting on the balcony, cooing and giggling together. Jean's taken some of my tranquillizers to relax, she tells me, do you want some too. No thanks, I say, and withdraw into the room, and at that moment I retreat from the pair of them in another sense as well. I don't mention Jean to Anna's girlfriend and I find ways to rationalize my silence to myself, this is a weightless holiday romance, nothing more, he's leaving in a few days, perhaps it will even be good for her. And who could take Jean seriously, a sad-looking cadaverous man full of melancholic vacancy, who speaks platitudes in a sonorous voice. Back home in Paris he's a builder by profession, but he does sculpture on the side. He claims he once danced with Nureyev.

This is what Anna's been looking for and she falls for him in a big way, suddenly it's all Jean this and Jean that, and then they're heading off on a rented scooter up the coast for a few days. I am very uneasy with this arrangement, I try to talk her out of it, but she laughs me off, I'm fine don't worry about me. And it's true that he is ceaselessly fretting over her, perhaps his concern is making things worse, maybe she'll be better if she has some time away from him. Mixed in with the mistrust is a good dose of relief too, it's pleasant to have her off my hands for a while. He hasn't come here, after all, just to be a chaperone, he's come to do some work, and in her absence he settles down to it, filling up pages with words. The plan is that we'll be doing some travelling ourselves when they get back, going down south together at the time of Jean's departure for home, so that very soon this peculiar interlude will be over.

Though it isn't so simple. The few days in Jean's company have sealed him in Anna's mind as her future and her fate. When she gets back she's full of crazy talk about moving to France to live, about having his child, and this talk will only get more fantastic as the rest of the trip goes on. The little romance has become a relationship, if only in her mind, and this despite the fact that he, Jean, refuses to become intimate with her. Her real life in Cape Town seems to have been annulled. More alarming is that Jean seems to have no idea of how ill she is, he treats her condition as a bad drama that's been foisted on her by manipulative people, you must just believe in yourself, he's been telling her, and you'll get better, you don't need to be taking all these pills. She repeats these insights wistfully, hoping that I'll agree, but what she doesn't tell me is that he's also been feeding her hash and cocaine and huge amounts of alcohol. She is noticeably looser when she returns, more obviously frayed at the edges, and this dissolution seems to feel like freedom to her, something she must pursue in order to get well.

In this dangerous state we head off, leaving Jean and Goa behind. I have some misguided notion that movement might be good for her, that the feeling of life passing by might suspend her internal clamour. And things are all right at first. There are a few days in Cochin, a cruise on the Kerala backwaters. But by the time they arrive in Varkala, a clifftop town far to the south, the strain between them is beginning to tell. Anna has to be ceaselessly attended to or she lapses into depression. She can't sit still for even a few minutes without becoming profoundly agitated. She's always breaking things or bumping into furniture or falling down. The talk about Jean is incessant and insane. Likewise the unpacking and repacking of her rucksack, which has long since lost its amusement value. When she's left alone for even a short while she gets into potentially harmful interactions with strangers along the way. On one occasion, for example, she has a physical fight with a peculiar Swiss woman who's mistreating a kitten on the beach, and another time she allows a shifty-looking older man, staying at the same hotel, to give her a body massage in his room.

In all of this he is constantly running behind, anxiously cleaning up or checking on her. He has begun to feel like a querulous maiden aunt, always worried and unhappy, and she has started to play the other part, of the innocent unfairly put upon, her wide eyes startled at the upset. Under the actual words they speak another dialogue is in progress, in which she is somehow a victim and I the nagging bully. I don't like this role, I try to pull back from it, and there are times when I am genuinely unsure which of us is out of touch. Besides which, he's afraid of a moment of truth, because he has no real power over her. If he tries to exert his authority and she refuses to obey, well, what could he do about that. If she walks out the door with her bag, telling him to get lost, he would have no recourse but to plead. Then they might both see where the power lies.

It's begun to feel to him as if a stranger has taken up residence in her, somebody dark and reckless that he doesn't trust, who wants to consume Anna completely. This stranger is still cautious, still biding her time. Meanwhile the person that he knows is visible, and sometimes in the ascendant. Then he can speak reasonably to her and feel that she is hearing, or laugh with her about something funny, or enlist her on his side. But the dark stranger always appears again, peering slyly over her shoulder, doing something alarming, and the softer Anna shrinks away. At moments the pair of them are there together, the sister-Anna and her scary twin, and they jostle each other for the upper hand. It's an uneven battle, the stranger is certainly stronger, but I keep hoping the pills will vanquish her.

I'm not a patient man by nature and the struggle is exhausting. My tolerance reaches a tipping point one afternoon when she wanders in from the beach, her face slack and empty. I stare at her for a moment, then ask quietly, are you stoned.

Yes, she says, smiling. Some guy out there offered me a toke.

He loses his temper. There has been irritation and upset till now, but this is something else, an explosion fuelled by despair. That's it, I tell her, you've broken every promise you made, you've broken our trust in you. This wasn't supposed to be a holiday, you were supposed to be working on yourself, now look what's happened. I'm taking you to Bombay tomorrow and sending you home.

The anger is real but the words are a bluff, even as he speaks he knows that he can't follow through. This is high season, the flights are very full, there is almost no chance she'd get a seat. But even if it could be arranged he can hear the nagging aunt in himself again, how churlish and unreasonable it sounds, sending her home two weeks early for puffing on a joint.

She weeps like a child, but his heart stays closed to her, the reserves of empathy are running out. When this raw exchange is over both of them feel empty, and it's still in a state of hollowness the next morning that he decides to make her an offer. No drugs of any kind, except those that have been prescribed for her, and only one drink a day. Any deviation from this agreement and he will carry out his threat. Is it a deal, he asks.

Her numb face nods slowly. It's a deal.

Shake on it, I say, and we clasp hands. This is not a renewal of friendship, it's a formal gesture of commitment, a contract that binds them both. But it feels as if he's claimed a victory, however small, over the bad other person inside her.

They go on to Madurai, where there is a spectacular temple he imagines she might like to photograph. He's seen the temple and all the other stops on their journey before, he has planned this route only for her, he wants to give her an enjoyable time and distract her from herself. But an increasing desperation underlies this enterprise, nothing holds her attention for long. She rushes through the temple and almost immediately falls into frenzy again. This is making me depressed, she says, let's go somewhere else. They visit a flower market and move on to a museum, but the effect is the same. Eventually he can't take it any more. I can't run around like this, he says, you go where you want to, I'll meet you at the station later.

They are booked on an overnight train to Bangalore. They have left their luggage at the station cloakroom that morning, and when he meets her there in the late afternoon she's repacking her rucksack and crying. We have to talk about what's happening between us, she says. I don't have anything to say, he answers wearily, and for the first time this is true. There is a fatal coldness in him towards her by now, he makes murmurous gestures of support, but his heart is vacant and she knows it. For some reason this tiny incident undoes her, she cries and cries without stopping, while he stares into space. He is just very tired, too tired to comfort her right now, perhaps tomorrow he will be strong enough again, and this is a crucial difference between them, he thinks in terms of tomorrow and the day after that, but for her there is only now, which is eternity.

Even on the train she continues to cry. Then she seems to reach a point of resolution and pulls herself together. She takes out her rucksack and starts her rummaging around. None of this is unusual, until she suddenly turns to him with panic in her eyes.

What is it.

My pills, she says. They're not here. They're gone. Somebody's stolen them.

What do you mean, they must be there, look again.

She's unpacking the rucksack now, the whole carriage is watching the scene. No, they're not here, somebody's stolen them, and she glares around wildly as if the culprit is right there.

The absurdity of the idea only strikes me by degrees. Who would steal your medicine, Anna. What would be the point.

I don't know, but. Then her face changes shape as something else occurs to her. Wait. No, I remember now. I took them out at the station while I was packing my bag.

You left them there.

I think so. In the cloakroom.

They stare at each other, while the tremendous mass of the train rushes on, every click of the wheels putting more distance between Anna and the medicine that has been holding her life together. This is a disaster, and the knowledge spreads across her face in a fresh upwelling of tears. Oh my God what will we do now.

The gulf between them has closed, he is joined with her in a flurry of high emotion. If she did leave the pills in the cloakroom there is a slim chance they might still be there. You're sure, Anna, you're sure that's where they are.

Yes, yes, I'm certain. She is wailing now, a spectacular display of distress, and everybody in the compartment has gathered around. There is jabbering and commotion. Somebody calls the conductor. He listens gravely to the story, then throws up his hands, nothing he can do about their problem.

But Anna is insistent, she won't let up. I will die without my medicine, she cries dramatically, and this persuades the hapless conductor to stop the train. At some nameless siding in the middle of the night the whole chain of carriages comes juddering to a halt and Anna descends with the uniformed man in tow and they go down the platform to find a phone, while I sit guarding the luggage. People hang out of the windows, watching and commenting. Others come to question me, what is the problem, why is your lady friend crying. It's as if her chaos has leaked out somehow and touched the physical world, throwing people and objects into disarray.

When she comes back there is still no clear answer. The cloakroom has been closed for the night, perhaps the medicine is there, perhaps not. As if to underline their uncertainty, the train starts to move again, a slow and noisy acceleration into the dark. I sit, pondering. Maybe it would be better to jump out at the next station and try to retrace our steps. Or maybe it would be better to go all the way to Bangalore, which is a major centre, and try to get some help there. What's not in doubt is that she's dependent on that little assortment of pills and if this is how mad she's been when she's taking them he doesn't want to think about how she'll be without them.

At this point a kindly avuncular man, who's been sitting opposite them since the start of the journey, speaks up. He is Mr. Hariramamurthy, he tells us, and perhaps he can be of assistance. He is going to a station near Bangalore but he will come to the last stop with us and speak to the railway police there, he's sure they'll be able to help.

No doubt these are merely polite words, when we get to the other end Mr. Hariramamurthy will have disappeared. But when we pull in to Bangalore the next morning there he is, standing by, ready to assist. Like helpless children we trail along behind him as he bustles from office to office, having complicated conversations with various functionaries, none of whom want to be bothered with our case. But Mr. Hariramamurthy is not deterred. There are retiring rooms upstairs at the station, he tells us, take one of these rooms and call me in two hours on this number. He hands us his card.

We manage to get a room. It seems like a reasonable option, the next train back to Madurai is this evening, if we have no solution by then we will make the journey. But when I ring Mr. Hariramamurthy later in the morning he tells us he has good news. His cousin works for the railways in some capacity, and has managed to track down the medicine. It will be sent on the train tonight and we have only to wait in our room, it will be delivered to the door.

This seems too good to be true, I am full of unworthy suspicion, surely we're being set up somehow. But we have no choice except to wait. We will be vigilant, whatever the scam is we won't fall for it, at the very worst we'll have lost a day, we can always go back tomorrow.

In the meanwhile they go into Bangalore and wander around. Anna is more manic than he has ever seen her, she fizzes and fiddles without stopping, her conversation jumping from one topic to another, how she's not ready to go back to South Africa yet, how she's almost sure her relationship at home is over, everything depends on Jean now, if she asks him maybe he'll come back to Goa and meet her before she goes home. Anna, I say, that's crazy, he's only just got back to France himself. She looks at me with wide, confused eyes, and in her stare I can see that she's lost all sense of time.

At some point in that long day, perhaps in the street, perhaps when they get back to the room, she says it. The revelation comes casually, without weight or significance, but it wipes out the surrounding world. You know, I was going to kill myself on the train.

What.

That's why I was looking for the medication. I was going to take all of it, then lie down to sleep.

You're not serious.

Yes, I am.

We look at each other and I see how serious she is.

But why, I say, why.

She shrugs and laughs. Since this crisis broke some of their old closeness has returned, in their room upstairs at the station they have guffawed uproariously at the sound of the train timetables being broadcast over speakers downstairs, it's all too absurd to be taken seriously. That morning in town she'd bought him a book in which she'd written, I love you very much my friend, and the words had felt renewed and true. Everything that has weighed them down has lifted, there is a lightness to their companionship that goes back many years, so that both of them seem stunned by the announcement she's just made. I don't know, she says, puzzled.

I suddenly felt like dying.

He can't answer this immediately, perhaps he never can. Ever since he's known her there's been this talk about killing herself one day. It never comes up in a dramatic way, more as a casual aside in conversation. He remembers asking her, for example, how she imagines she might look when she grows old, to which she immediately replies that she never will be old. She is always planning her funeral, telling her friends to play this piece of music, or to have the service in that particular church, and her tone at these moments suggests that she herself will be present, a spectator at the event. It's hard not to feel manipulated when she speaks like this, and it's hard, too, to feel constantly alarmed by a threat you've heard so many times over. Besides which, why would somebody like Anna, in perfect physical health, loved and admired and desired by so many people, want to die. There's no plausible reason, so that even now, when he can see that she means it, he can't quite get a hold on what she says. And in any case she's instantly off on some fresh upheaval, knocking over the lamp or losing the keys to the room, and it all becomes one ongoing crisis he's trying to contain. That's how it is with Anna, death at one moment, farce the next, and it's hard sometimes to distinguish between the two.

It's a couple of days before he can bring himself to speak about it and even then he does so tentatively, approaching the question in a circle. Did you think about what you were doing to me, he asks her. Did you think about what it would be like for me to be left alone with your dead body in India.

She considers the matter seriously for a while, then nods. Point taken, she says.

Incredibly, the medicine arrives in the morning. There's a knock on the door and a man is standing outside, holding the little black bag. Anna seizes it from him, her relief is like joy, the means of her death feels like life to her today.

Now they can resume their journey and after leaving effusive messages of thanks for Mr. Hariramamurthy they travel on to Hampi. This is a day away from their starting point in Goa, to which they still intend to return, but meanwhile they plan a short sojourn in this extraordinary site. The ruins of an ancient Hindu empire spread across a massive landscape of boulders and weird hills, like a kind of ruin in itself. You could spend days here, just wandering, but almost immediately the recent equanimity starts to unravel. Anna can't cope with the setting, the desolation echoes something in her, she's soon back in her familiar pattern. No sooner have they arrived at one spot than she wants to rush on to the next, nothing contains her, nothing holds her in. This place is shit, she tells him, I want to go back to Goa.

There's nothing for it but to cut the stay short. He books tickets on the train for the next day. They're only due to leave at nine in the morning, but she's already up at five o'clock, making a racket as she tries to open the door, and he loses his cool with her. For God's sake, why don't you take your sleeping pills at night. Because I don't need them. But obviously you do.

The train is a slow one, stopping at every station, and the long, hot hours pass mostly in silence, not the silence of companionship any more but of exhaustion, of some deep reserve that's been used up. There are two weeks left of this trip and he's resolved that they'll spend all of it in one spot, close to the beach, where she seems to feel more calm than elsewhere. After that he'll be free again, pursuing his own travels for another four months.

They arrive in the village after dark. The mood in the downstairs restaurant at the hotel is festive and the merriment infects them. They have dinner with some of the other guests and it's as if they never left. That night they sleep in the same room upstairs, in the same bed, and the big looping journey they've made is just one more completed circle, bringing them back to exactly the same point.

The next morning she wakes him before dawn again, banging around in the dark. It's a repeat of the previous day, though only he remembers it. What do you want me to do, she cries, if I'm awake I'm awake. I want you to take your sleeping pills, he says, that's why you've got them, isn't it. He's too cross to sleep again, so he gets up, scratchy with tiredness, and goes for a long walk on the beach. When he gets back she's sitting downstairs having breakfast, but he doesn't join her, why exactly I can't say. Would it make any difference to what follows, perhaps it would, perhaps everything comes down to one silence too many. He sits at a table by himself, like a stranger, and when he's done he comes over. I'm going to Margao, I tell her. To do some shopping.

She nods, I still recall the blue stare of her eyes.

He catches a bus into Margao and spends an hour at the shops. When he gets back to the room at mid-morning the door is locked from the inside. She opens when he knocks and then retreats to the bed. He notices that she's wearing her nightdress over her bikini and next to her is a half-finished bottle of beer, as well as a small teddy bear she's carried everywhere with her for comfort.

Were you sleeping.

I had a swim earlier, I feel tired.

There's a curious feeling in the room, the spiky angles of confrontation that filled their earlier exchange have gone, she seems soft and somehow younger, as if she's retreated into childhood. The curtains have been drawn and there's a stillness over everything, completely at odds with the time of day. In retrospect these signs are obvious, so obvious that they constitute a signal, and it's an indication of how worn out he is, how lost in the endless repetitions of the scenario, that he doesn't understand. Afterwards he will blame himself, he blames himself even now, for his failure to see what is plainly in front of him.

I got an e-mail from home, she says drowsily.

About what.

She thinks the medicine isn't working. She thinks I should go back early.

And you don't want to.

No, I know what that means. They'll put me in the clinic again.

We can talk about it, Anna, I say, but not when you're half asleep. Come and speak to me outside.

I get a book and go and sit on the balcony in the sun. My anger towards her has dissipated, I feel the weary resumption of duty. But she doesn't come out to join me. I hear furtive activity inside, the noise of crinkling papers, maybe only a plastic bag being disturbed by the leisurely rotation of the fan, and the sound of her lighting a cigarette. Later her breathing slows and deepens. I read for a while, then get up and stretch, thinking about heading to the beach, but when I step into the room I see a pile of dirty clothes in need of washing and take it to the bathroom. Once the clothes are rinsed and wrung out and spread on the railing to dry, perhaps an hour has gone by.

It's a chance conjunction of images that finally draws the picture together. As I bend down to put away the washing powder, I happen to glance sideways and see Anna on top of the bed and on the floor underneath it a heap of discarded medicine wrappers. Her pills. Her sleeping body. It's those wrappers that made the crinkling noise I heard, an insistent scratching and rustling that has picked at my mind, bothering me. There has been something in the scene that isn't right, something that I know without knowing, and when the realization arrives at last it's like a coldness rising from my core that dispels the warm day outside. No, I say aloud, it can't be. Yes, I think, she's done it.

Now I'm watching myself move, like somebody who isn't me. See him run around the bed and grab her by the arm and shake her. Hear him calling out her name. And when she doesn't wake, when her eyelids flicker slightly and close again, the last doubt has gone. Now he understands that this has been coming all along, right from day one. How could you not have known, why did you not act weeks ago while there was still time, how could you have arrived at a moment like this when all the warnings were in place.

There are no words for what is happening now, for what he thinks and feels. His body is working by itself, trying to undo what is already accomplished, while his mind and spirit are elsewhere, having a high, disconnected dialogue. What will happen if, if what, if she, no, I don't want to think about that. Act, act, do something. See him grab the woman in the bed and drag her into a sitting position and slap her hard across the face. Anna, wake up, you must wake up. And finally she does, her eyes open properly at last. Her expression is stunned. Listen to me, he says. You must tell me. What have you done.

She thinks for a little while, then whispers. I ate my medicine.

How many pills did you take.

All of them.

All of them. He knows, with some separate, rational part of his brain, what the mathematics are. About two hundred tranquillizers and fifty sleeping pills. A white cloud of terror drains the colour out of everything. See him run from the room and down the stairs, hear him shouting to the waiter in the restaurant, his voice something separate from him, is there a doctor in the village, call the doctor right now. There are a few diners at the tables, they stir with alarm and curiosity as they watch him turn and pound back up the stairs again. He drags her off the bed and onto her feet. You must move, Anna, you have to keep moving. Think, think. Vomit the pills. He takes her into the bathroom, bends her over the toilet, sticks his fingers down her throat. Her head lolls heavily on her neck. Vomit, Anna, bring them up. He takes his toothbrush, uses the handle to press her tongue down. She retches dryly, nothing comes up. I'm begging you, do it, Anna, do it. She is collapsing, sliding sideways against the wall. Got to keep moving. He walks her back into the other room and up and down the floor, stopping to stick his fingers into her mouth as if by force he can retrieve the seeds of death she's taken into herself. Vomit, Anna, for Christ's sake how could you do this to yourself and to me, and here of all places, where there is nobody to help.

He has never felt so alone. But in that moment somebody else is there. An older woman from England, who lives in a private house on the property for half of the year. He hardly knows her, bar a few brief conversations, but he feels overwhelmingly, desperately glad to see her.

Is everything all right here, she asks in a small voice.

He realizes now that he's been shouting with all his force, signalling his distress in rings of sound that move outwards from the room. Caroline, he says, oh Caroline. You have to help me. What's wrong, what has she done. She's overdosed, she's taken her medicine. Two hundred and fifty pills, he says, amazed at the figure all over again.

She is much calmer than he is and she brings an air of cool authority into the room. He remembers vaguely that she's a nurse back in her other life in England, and he's happy to defer to her when she takes charge. Salt water, she says, we must have salt water. I rush out to the restaurant and come back with two litres of warm, salty water, which we pour into Anna, pinching her nose closed to force her to swallow. Then Caroline goes outside and returns with a long reed she's broken off somewhere. While I hold Anna's head back, her mouth open, Caroline forces the reed down her throat. They are working as a team now, two midwives trying to coax a birth, but though the reed goes all the way down, so deep that it comes up with blood on the tip, nothing happens. Their patient is passive, neither helping nor hindering them, but her passivity is like a sort of defiance, from beyond which she watches with amusement. Look at all your striving, too late, too late.

By now it's clear that the doctor isn't coming. Somebody calls a taxi and they half-help, half-carry her down the stairs. A crowd has gathered at a respectful distance, watching the drama. We get into the car, all three of us on the back seat, Anna in the middle with a bucket between her knees. As we drive to Margao, with the car repeatedly stalling and struggling to start again, a bizarre conversation unfolds. Why did you do this. Because I want to die. What reason do you have to die. What reason do I have to live. You are a very selfish girl, Caroline announces firmly.

By now Anna has almost lost consciousness, she is swaying and slurring. We discuss where to take her, there is a private doctor nearby, but we decide to go to the government hospital, perhaps their facilities will be better. We have to carry her in when we arrive and load her onto a trolley like a sack of meat. While we are explaining to the doctor what she's done, the taxi driver appears, plucking at my sleeve. Seven hundred rupees, he insists, about five times the going rate, but I hurl the money at him, this is no time for argument. Anna is signalling weakly to me and when I bend over her she whispers something inaudible. What are you saying, I can't hear you. She forms the words again and this time I do hear. Tell them what I've taken. I have told them, I say, just as she slips away into unconsciousness.

I've brought the prescription for the medicine with me to show the doctor and he shakes his head over it. She took all of this. All of it, yes. He must do a stomach pump, he says, and he explains the hospital policy to me. It is extraordinary, he has to repeat it before I fully understand. The treatment, the hospital, are free, though the equipment and drugs are not. But it's not possible simply to pay for them, they must also physically be bought. So the doctor writes his requirements on a slip of paper, which I must then carry down the corridor, across a courtyard, down another corridor to the pharmacy. A small mob of people jostles in front of the counter, each of them waving their slip of paper, each of them shouting to be heard. I plunge into the crowd, hacking a path with my elbows to the front. My friend is dying, I roar, please help me first.

Maybe the note in my voice reaches them, because they take my slip of paper promptly. There's a short wait while the bored attendant wanders between the shelves, picking out what is required. A length of tube, a saline solution, some gauze. Then it's all totalled up, my money is taken, the change is laboriously counted. A sense of unreality has thickened the air, like a dream in which you cannot move, and through this fog I run back up the corridor, across the courtyard, down the next corridor to the room. A surly nurse takes the equipment and pushes the tube down Anna's throat. The saline solution is pumped in, then sucked back out again. I peer at it hopefully, expectantly, looking for the load of pills, but the fluid is clear.

Nothing, the nurse says. Her stomach is empty.

That isn't possible.

Look, she says, and performs the operation again. The receptacle fills with its liquid. The nurse slouches off to do something else, leaving the tube in place. Caroline eyes it suspiciously.

I don't think that's in her stomach, she says.

What do you mean.

I think she's put it into her lung. We both stare at the tube. After a moment, Caroline says, I'm going to take it out. She steps forward and pulls the tube from Anna's throat and at this instant the nurse reappears, shrieking furiously. When Caroline tries to explain she shakes her head, the tube was in her stomach, she insists, don't tell me my job.

But Caroline is right, later that day they will have to drain Anna's lung and later still she will develop pneumonia on that side. But all of this is in the future and where they are is very much the present tense. They have moved her upstairs to do a stomach wash, the ingredients for which I again have to rush and buy at the pharmacy. Afterwards I'm detained downstairs by the doctor. He's telling me that if the stomach wash doesn't do the job, they will have to move her to the big hospital in Panjim. They have a heart and lung machine there, she is in danger of organ failure, they just don't have the equipment here in Margao.

By the time I get upstairs and find her, another scene has developed. She is lying in a bed in a ward full of sick women, a thicket of ailing female flesh. They are all Indian and the peculiar drama unfolding in the corner with its cast of foreigners is of intense interest to them. They stare with candid fascination as it becomes clear that the stomach wash has made the sleeping woman's bowels give way. A stain spreads across the back of her nightdress, a bad smell rises. He looks around wildly in search of a nurse, but of course it doesn't work like this. The doctor tells us sternly, your friend has made a mess. You must clean it.

Oh God, I say, I can't believe this. And it's one of the few occasions in his life when the statement is actually true. This morning I was walking on the beach, now I must clean my dying friend's shit. Caroline takes control again, becoming terse and efficient. We'll need rubber gloves and disinfectant and cotton wool. The doctor writes these items on a piece of paper, I run down two flights of stairs and across the hospital to the pharmacy. When I get back Caroline has cut Anna's nightdress off her, as well as the swimming costume underneath. We roll her onto her side. She is an absolutely unhelpful mass, a dead weight. The other women in the ward find this whole exercise hilarious, they giggle and titter behind their hands.

As we start on the business of cleaning her, it rapidly becomes too much. I put the cotton swab down and say, more to myself than anybody, I don't know if I can do this. Caroline looks at me and says, let me handle it, I do it as part of my job. As a nurse, she takes care of sick, elderly, often bed-ridden people in England, which is how she makes her money to stay in India. Again I have that rush of gratitude to Caroline, for undertaking this task instead of me.

The watching women rock with merriment as Caroline wipes her clean. I go out into the corridor. I feel far from myself and from the surfaces around me, as if I'm looking down a long dark tunnel at the sunlit world beyond. The doctor, a fat lazy-looking man, comes back. We're going to have to move her, he says. But not like that.

What do you mean.

She is naked, no. She must be dressed. We cannot take her in the ambulance like that.

But, I say. But. I don't have a dress. Can't you, I mean, don't you have something, a hospital gown or something.

He shakes his head. You must find a dress.

It's hard to believe, under the circumstances, that modesty should be a priority. I want to seize this plump, complacent man, who seems almost to be enjoying my plight, and shake him till his teeth rattle and he concedes that a dress doesn't matter, no not at all, at a moment like this. But I know I have no choice. See him rush down the stairs again, along the corridor, out the door to the hospital and along the street to the main road. He goes into a shop, but they don't sell dresses. For that, they tell him helpfully, he will have to go to the market. So he runs out again and flags down a bus and pays to get on, like any ordinary passenger. See him ride across town to the market, a point of unnatural stillness at the centre of so much flux and movement, and then explode from the bus, rushing from shop to shop, a dress, I must have a dress. Eventually he finds one and pays and flees without waiting for change. Outside there is a man sitting idly on a motorbike, I grab him by the arm. Please, I cry, please take me to the hospital, I'll pay you, just take me. Sensing the panic, or eager for money, the man bears me away on his little machine, weaving through the traffic.

Back at the hospital he pays the man and runs upstairs. Nothing has changed, Anna still lies in the same position, her naked back to the room. We drag and haul her into the dress and no sooner have we succeeded than she shits in it again. It's too bad, I say, she'll have to stay like that. The chorus of women falls about in laughter.

There is an ambulance standing by to take her to Panjim. It's a drive of an hour and perhaps an hour has elapsed since our arrival here.

These stretches of time feel like huge distances, a desert stretching in both directions. By now he knows the score, he will have to supply everything at Panjim, he has to get money and clothes. Before he can even voice the suggestion Caroline has picked up on it, let me ride with her, she says, you go to the room and fetch what you need.

It feels as if he last saw the room a long time in the past, not just a few hours ago. He collects a bag of clothes and some money and is about to leave when he notices Anna's journal lying on the bed. She has been writing in it obsessively since the journey started, apparently documenting every moment of the trip, and he wonders now if any final message has been penned there. And when he turns with dread to the last pages, there it is, in a big incoherent scrawl. Damon do NOT feel guilty. I know if I go back I will be admitted. Rather die at a high point in my life. On the facing page, another note. Dear Everyone I Love, I cannot live with my illness any more. It is no one's fault. I love you all and will see you in another lifetime.

There is more, instructions about what to do with her body and money and possessions, some messages to her girlfriend and family and also to Jean. But all of it is written in the same frantic way, spilling all over the page, seemingly under high pressure. He thinks she scribbled it down after she'd swallowed the pills, maybe even while he was sitting outside reading, as the shutters started to come down in her mind.

He closes the book and puts it away, no time to follow this now. Before he can go to the hospital there is a call he must make, a call he's dreading, to Anna's lover in Cape Town. What he has to tell her is everything she most dreads and fears, everything she's worked against for the past eight years. He goes to the public phone booth at the crossroads and dials. He can't get through and can't get through and then he reaches the answering machine. But what can he say, there are no words, least of all words to be spoken onto tape. So the message he leaves is bare and basic, just the facts and the number of the hotel. Then there is a silence before he ends off in a different voice, I don't know what to tell you, it's not looking good.

The owner of the hotel has offered to drive me to Panjim. I sit silently next to this bald, glowering, middle-aged man, who has dressed up in a blue suit for the occasion, as we travel northward for an hour in his jeep. The hospital is a complex of peeling concrete buildings, looking more like tenement blocks than an institution, on the very edge of the city. Brown bushy scrub, reminding him of Africa, spreads away beyond the perimeter wall.

Anna is still in arrivals, she hasn't been admitted yet. Caroline is sitting on a bench in the passage outside, looking stricken and sad. The air of assured authority she wore earlier has gone. It will be a while before I discover that the ride in the ambulance with Anna's inert body has stirred things up for Caroline, things that have nothing to do with where we are now.

I'm sorry, she says in a low voice, but I think your friend is dying.

She means I must prepare myself, but how do you prepare for this. When I go into the ward I have to walk through a crowd of horizontal patients in crisis before I find Anna. She's an alarming blue colour and sucking air from an oxygen canister with a hoarse, noisy effort. An arrogant doctor is strutting about, dispensing opinions like favours, and when I ask him what her chances are he waves his hand airily. She must go to ICU, he says, then we will see.

Soon afterwards she's admitted to the ICU ward upstairs and suddenly all the commotion comes to a stop, converted into the painful stillness of waiting. Anna is behind a closed door, out of sight, and the rest of us must sit outside, in a dirty room full of plastic chairs. The attention is all on that door, which hardly ever opens. When it does it's usually to allow a nurse or doctor out, who will call the name of a patient aloud. When Anna's name is called, which it often is on that first day, I must run with the script in hand to a separate wing of the hospital, to the familiar scene of clamour and struggle in the pharmacy, and return with whatever drugs or emergency equipment are required, and these missions are a relief from the waiting.

It dawns on me very quickly that, without anybody to help, I can never leave this room. Every hour of every day somebody must be on hand. My dismay at this prospect is tempered when I start speaking to a few of the other people around me, the stories in that room put my own plight into perspective. One family has been taking it in turns, relieving each other in six hour shifts, for months. One woman, who has nobody to assist her, has been literally living there with a bag of clothes and a toothbrush, for five weeks and no end in sight.

Caroline has gone back to the village with the hotel owner and the night yawns away in front of me like a black and empty space. But not long afterwards a Dutch tourist by the name of Sjef arrives, whom I know a little from the past two seasons. He's come to take over for the night, he says, so that I can go home and sleep. His kindness makes me cry, but I can't bring myself to leave. It's my expectation, though I don't say it aloud, that my friend will die tonight and I want to be here when it happens.

So Sjef and I undertake this first vigil together. At eight o'clock, to my surprise, there's a stirring in the room, everybody gathering around the door of the ward. What's going on, I ask, and somebody explains that twice a day, in the night and the morning, the friends and family of patients are allowed inside for five minutes. So we pass into the inner sanctum, with its two rows of beds and its atmosphere of spectral suspension. Anna is on a heart-lung machine, with all kinds of tubes and wires pushed into her. Her face has returned to its normal colour, but in the midst of so much humming technology she herself seems lifeless, a form wrapped around emptiness, a version of the corpse she wants so badly to be.

I touch her hand and whisper to her. You have to fight, I tell her, you have to come back to us. There's no response at all, and then a nurse walks briskly through, ushering us out.

That first night is very long and almost sleepless. Aside from the missions to the pharmacy, the hours pass in a tedium under the fluorescent lights. The bathroom which everyone must share is filthy, and has two bins overflowing with hospital refuse from which rats scatter in all directions every time the door is opened. When he eventually lies down on the floor to sleep, he puts screws of newspaper into his ears to stop the ubiquitous cockroaches from crawling in.

But morning returns eventually and the door is opened again. Anna is lying exactly as she was last night, a princess frozen by a witch's spell. For her there is no dirty floor to endure, no passing time, no rats or insects, these elements belong to the rest of us, and to the days that follow. But I'm rescued by Caroline and by Sjef and his English wife Paula, who between them take turns helping me stand guard outside the door. We ride back and forth between the village and the hospital, an hour each way, in overlapping shifts.

The time I spend in the village is mostly occupied with e-mails and phone calls, messages both personal and official stitching across the sea. The biggest ongoing conversation is with Anna's girlfriend in Cape Town. The devastation is enormous. I can feel her helplessness from the other side of the world, a witness who's not even present. Of course she wants to come over immediately. But the practicalities are complicated, there is the visa, which will take a few days to organize, and also the flights are still full. But I try to dissuade her for another reason as well. It would be terrible for her to come here, only to discover that Anna doesn't want her but somebody else instead. The memory of the last few weeks is still heavily with me, all the talk about Jean, her knight in shining armour, who has expressed no interest in rushing to her side, even though he's been told what's happened. He's still a secret, but eventually I have to speak. There is something, I say, something I have to tell you.

Yes.

Anna had an affair over here.

There is a silence. I knew, she says at last, I knew it.

I'm sorry.

With a man.

Yes. She was determined to do it, I say, and any man would do. I'm sorry I couldn't tell you before. But I thought you should know about it before you come out here. She's been saying her relationship with you is over, that she wants to be with this guy.

Now I spill out all the details, everything that's been kept under wraps. We seem to have arrived at some confessional core, where there are no more secrets, no more concealments. We are turning ourselves inside out, as if the truth might absolve us, but it only brings more pain. It may be in this conversation, or perhaps in another soon afterwards, that I walk with the phone into the middle of an empty field next to the hotel and bawl. I'm sorry, I tell her, I'm sorry I said I could look after her, I had no idea what I was taking on.

He returns to Anna's journal and spends hours reading it, from the very first page. He feels no compunction about delving into her private thoughts and feelings, if she has brought us to this moment of truth, well, let it embrace her too. What he finds there is sad and shocking. It's as he realized in the end, her act was not a momentary impulse, on the contrary, it was a goal she yearned for from the outset, one she worked herself up to by degrees. Her girlfriend has meanwhile discovered, hidden in their home somewhere, a letter that Anna left behind before her departure. It's almost, but not quite, a suicide note, further proof that her plans were made far in advance. So she was never on their side, on the side of everybody who loved her and tried to make her well. Instead she was in league with the dark other stranger inside her, the one who wants her dead. It's hard not to feel profoundly betrayed. Even as they made plans for the trip, with all the talk about how good it would be for her, she was already dreaming up this other scenario, in which she needed him as the helpless bystander, the custodian of her remains. If she recovers, which it begins to seem she might, he doesn't know how he will ever be able to speak to her again.

Meanwhile he sweeps up the litter of discarded medicine wrappers from under the bed. It's painful to be reminded every time he's in the room, but there is another reason for this clean-up. Attempted suicide is a crime in India and there could be more serious trouble coming. When she was first admitted to the hospital in Margao, a policeman stationed at the emergency room came to speak to him and take his details. And at the hospital in Panjim a doctor approaches Sjef one day and tells him, if there is any hassle from the authorities, to give him a call.

In preparation for possible trouble, he speaks to the South African embassy in Bombay, giving them all the details of what happened and emphasizing, in advance, that the drugs she took were of a legal nature. But he also knows by now from her journal that she was indulging in other drugs with Jean, so in case of an unexpected search he goes through Anna's rucksack from top to bottom, to be sure there's nothing incriminating.

Around me, in the village where I have spent months of my life and come to know some of the locals quite well, there has descended a general air of suspicion. A number of people, some of them near strangers, have felt free to question me aggressively about what took place. A few pretend sympathy, but it always leads to the same point. Your girlfriend, they say, why did she do it. Were you fighting with her. The inference is clear, and chimes exactly with my underlying guilt. She's not my girlfriend, I begin, but I always fall silent. My protests only confirm what they believe.

So I retreat into a tiny circle of refuge. Caroline and Sjef and Paula are my new and only friends. I spend a lot of time in their company and we talk endlessly about what happened and what might still be coming. We even manage to laugh at certain moments. I really want her to recover, I say one day, so that I can kill her myself.

It's around now that I become aware something else is afoot, something connected to Caroline. I hardly know her, yet we've been plunged into artificial intimacy, and in our scattered conversations I've learned a little bit about her. She's mentioned that she was married but that her husband was killed in an accident long ago in Morocco. I gather, between the lines, that this is the central event of her life, one which has marked her deeply, despite the intervening time, and what's happened now with Anna seems to have revived the memory for her again. She talks about it now and then, always in sideways allusive terms, but a shadow creeps over her face, her eyes fill up with tears. That ride in the ambulance with Anna, she says one day, it was terrible, it reminded me of, oh never mind. On another occasion she says, I've been having the most terrible dreams, all about what happened in Morocco. She doesn't go on, but on the far side of her words I sense a chasm falling away into darkness, and I don't want to look over the edge.

On the third day already there are signs of life. Anna makes the occasional movement, her eyelids flicker, and on the fourth day she's awake. When I go through for the morning visit, she peers dimly at me and her mouth, stretched around a thick plastic tube, manages a smile. When I visit again that evening the tube is gone and she's lying there, whole and restored.

After everything that we've been through, this feels unreal. I stroke her hand and speak gently, a gentleness that in truth is almost genuine at this moment, as I ask her how it feels to be alive. She's very weak and I have to crane to catch her whispered reply. Shit, she says.

After this period of suspension and stasis, events start to move quickly again. First thing the next day they move her from ICU to the coronary ward opposite. They need the bed, one of the nurses explains, and she will be under intermediate care.

And at first this new arrangement seems in balance. Because she has no physical power, she's mostly docile and compliant, though she still requires constant care and attention and one of us must be on hand to provide it. For the first day or two she has terrible diarrhoea and every little while has to be helped out of the bed and steadied while she crouches over a bedpan. He remembers the conflicting sensations of pity and distaste as he holds her upright, his hands and feet being splattered with the watery discharge. She smiles sweetly up at him and murmurs, this is a test of our friendship. You have no idea, he answers.

Afterwards it's his duty to carry the brimming bedpan into the rat-infested bathroom and empty it out and wash it clean. It's a job he repeats over and over through the day, a humbling task which is more than has ever been asked of him before, but he does it without protest, maybe only because he has no choice. All around him are other people similarly engaged, and there is a resigned solidarity in their efforts.

At some point in the day she looks over at the next bed and whispers confidingly, look at that one, she's definitely in here for an eating disorder.

I glance across, perplexed. But she isn't a patient, Anna, she's a visitor.

Anna raises her head and peers. Well, she ought to be a patient, she says. She's enormous.

No, she isn't, I say, but before I can point out that the woman concerned is actually quite tiny, I break down in laughter. It's a mad conversation, but for the first time in many days the madness is almost charming. Underneath the words is a glimmer of the friend I remember, eccentric and funny rather than demented.

Sjef stays with her that night and I go back to the room. Relief at having emerged from the tunnel makes it possible for me to sleep properly, and it's in a state of semi-replenishment that I return to the hospital next morning. But even before I can cross the threshold of the ward I realize something is amiss. Sjef is waiting, he takes me grimly aside.

It's been a difficult night, he says.

Difficult. I glance across at where Anna is sitting up in bed, her arms folded crossly, glaring back at us. Don't worry, I'll deal with her, I say.

But nothing has prepared him for the transformation that's taken place. The sweet, feeble angel of yesterday has disappeared, to be replaced by something else completely. The dark stranger has waxed to the full. The first sign comes when he tries to talk to her about the way she's treated Sjef. You don't understand, she says. That's only half the story. The fucking bastard. The way he speaks to me.

He's spent the whole night looking after you.

Who asked him to. I don't need looking after.

You do, but in any case somebody has to be here. It's a hospital rule.

Why didn't you do it. Where were you.

I was at the room, trying to sleep. Please, Anna, it was the first chance I've had. Sjef was helping me, so that I could rest.

Rest from what. You're making a big fucking drama about

nothing. All I want is cigarettes, that fucking bastard won't buy them for me.

This is a coronary ward, you're not allowed to smoke in here.

Fuck that, I'll do what I fucking please. Go and get me cigarettes.

He looks at her, stunned. But before the conversation can go any further, she has another attack of diarrhoea. Help me, she orders, I have to go. There is the squatting down, the splattering. This is so horrible, she mutters. Horrible horrible horrible. It's not much fun for me either, I say.

Afterwards, while I empty the bedpan in the bathroom, I have an uneasy qualm about what she might be up to. Panic makes me slop the mess over my hands, and washing myself clean slows me even further. But my instinctive premonition is correct, when I get back to the ward Anna is out of bed and heading off somewhere. Her legs are still wobbly, or she would have covered more ground.

Where are you going.

To buy cigarettes.

I told you, it's not allowed, and anyway you have no money.

Take me back to the hotel. I'm fine now, I demand to leave this minute. It's unconstitutional to keep me against my will.

The constitution won't help you, this is India. And the more trouble you make, the longer you'll have to stay here. Now get back into bed.

Unexpectedly, she obeys, but when she's properly settled she says smugly, I wasn't going to buy cigarettes, I was going to throw myself out of the window.

There are bars on the windows and they're only on the first floor, but nevertheless he's filled with furious despair. He tries to control his voice as he says, we are doing everything we can to keep you alive.

Who asked you to. Just let me die. Walk away. I give you permission to just walk away.

I'm not doing this for you. I'm doing it for other people who love you. And for me, so that I can look myself in the eye.

Hah. She fixes a certain gaze on him, a disdainful calculating stare. This is all your fault, you know. You took responsibility for me when you brought me along, and look what happened.

She is not too ill to sight and hit my most vulnerable spot, the truth that will hurt me for ever. My voice is choked when I answer. And you, you're not responsible, I suppose. The fact is, you didn't care about anybody else, you just did what you wanted.

I couldn't, because you stopped me.

And I'll keep on stopping you. You're going back to South Africa alive and after that you're not my worry any more.

You're not worried about me anyway, you just care what other people will say.

Right now that's true. Right now I hate you.

So what, I hate you too.

These ugly words have come from a deep core in me, part of the destructive essence that Anna has pared us to. It takes an effort of will to understand, even in a theoretical way, how very sick she is. It will be years before I'm able to acknowledge that she is psychotic, her mania full-blown, with no medication to subdue her and with a raging fever from pneumonia, and even then it's hard to forgive her. Because from long ago, even in her sanest moments, she wanted this and worked hard to reach it, her toxic, terminal rapture. The rest of us are just walk-on parts in a drama centred only on her.

I remember every accusing word, including my own, like a knife in the guts, like something that has shamed us both. Yet she herself is untouched. Later that same day, for example, Sjef and Paula and Caroline all arrive together to help me. In an attempt to bring down her temperature we buy ice from the canteen downstairs and press it all over her body. She wails and protests but also smiles, look at me, she says, I have a whole team working on me, and in that moment she is angelic again, my coy and flirtatious friend, and the awful exchange of that morning has disappeared. She remembers none of it, nothing of what is said and done, even by herself. She floats above all the pain and grief and guilt that she's created, looking down on our scurrying and striving. There is a very real element of contempt in the way she treats us now, a quality of mocking laughter at our concern. She is far beyond us all, because she's not afraid of death any longer, which is both her weakness and her greatest strength.

And it only gets worse. Every day she is more powerful and wily, more resourceful in her self-destruction, and her demands become more insistent. I want my money-belt, she announces one morning, and when I tell her that I'm taking care of it she accuses me of stealing her money. Another time she wants her shoes. Look at me, she cries wretchedly, I have to sit here with nothing on my feet, you're so cruel to me. These appeals move him not at all, with money and shoes she will be able to escape, he knows what she's after. But when he refuses she starts to repeat it like an hysterical child, my money, give me my money, give me my shoes right now. He just keeps shaking his head. No. There is perverse pleasure in wielding that word, in being able to withhold death from her.

But he's also aware that time is short and that she might outplay him yet. In a few days Sjef and Paula will be going home and then only he and Caroline will be left. He doubts that between them they'll be able to keep her covered, it will mean shifts of twelve hours each, and she can't be trusted for a moment. She's out of bed and heading towards the door as soon as anyone's back is turned. He has spoken to the nurses at the desk and implored them to keep an eye, but they are busy and distracted and also not that interested, what do they care for this rude foreign woman and her over-wrought minders.

Most alarming of all, as her physical condition improves she is shunted to more general wards in the hospital. Fewer nurses are in attendance here and the wards are fuller. After three or four days she's taken to a room where two people are sharing each bed and some patients are lying on the floor. She begins to weep and rave, this is unacceptable, I refuse to stay here, I demand you take me out of this place.

He would like to comply, but it isn't so simple. She is supposed to pass through levels of medical assessment before she can be officially discharged, this process is not in his hands, and whenever he's asked about it the answer is always vague. A few days, they say.

We'll have to see. One doctor has told him that she will have to be psychologically evaluated, a prospect that terrifies him, if she's certified it may be a very long time before anybody can get her out. But even if he could remove her today, where would he take her. She cannot go back to the village. The flights are all full, he has already checked, he cannot send her home early. The best hope is to try to keep her here until the date of her original departure, which is about five days away by now. How she will be able to travel in this condition still remains to be seen.

But the chances of holding out till that flight home are slim. This is Sjef and Paula's last day, in the morning they will be gone. He and Caroline are worn to spiritual shreds by now and Anna is at her maddest and most powerful. It is the lowest point they've reached since she woke up and at this desperate moment another character enters from the wings, a sly and sidelong fellow in uniform who comes picking his way through the bodies on the floor. We look at him in bemusement.

He is very polite. He's from the casualty police, he tells us, and he'd like to be of assistance. As we must know, this is a matter for criminal investigation, and when Anna is discharged she will probably be detained. It's a difficult situation but if we speak to him, and at this point he gives us a piece of paper with his name and number on it, he's sure that we can come to some agreement.

Of all of us, Anna is the only one happy to see him. Oh thank God, she cries, at last, somebody who understands. All I want is to get out of here.

The seedy little man nods in sympathy. I will help you, he says.

Thank you, thank you.

I thank him too, more demurely, and shake his hand. But when he's slid away again like an insidious drop of oil, the rest of us look at each other despairingly. Oh bloody hell. What will we do now.

Paula speaks up. Remember that doctor who spoke to Sjef, she says, maybe you should contact him. Sjef isn't here today, he's at the room packing up their bags, but I shoot off to a payphone and ring him. Luckily he's kept the name and number of the doctor concerned and I'm able to call him immediately afterwards. He listens to the story and sighs. That's bad news, he tells me carefully, it's what I was worried about. Here's what you need to do, but you can't ever use my name or say that you spoke to me.

I won't.

The police must have been tracking her through the hospital, they know she's going to be discharged soon. That's when they'll grab you, so you must get her out before then. Do it now. Go to the doctor in charge of the ward and tell him you want a DAMA. That stands for discharge against medical advice. He'll argue and tell you it's impossible, but you must insist. Then take her out before the doctor can call the police and let them know. The doctor will also be getting a cut, so you must be fast.

But where will I take her. I have nowhere to go.

There is a private hospital in Panjim run by a friend of mine. Go and see him. His name is Dr. Ajoy.

He gives me the address of the hospital and I take a taxi over there immediately. It's a small, clean, quiet place, close to the beach, and Dr. Ajoy is helpful. Yes, he says, she can be accommodated. He has drugs to calm her down. I should bring her round now.

In a last co-ordinated burst of activity, we engineer the escape. The taxi driver who has been ferrying us all back and forth between the village and the hospital keeps his car at a side-entrance, waiting. Inside I go to the nurse in charge of the ward and ask to see the doctor on duty. He's not there, she tells me.

Where is he. He's supposed to be here, isn't he.

He's at a meeting.

Well, we're taking my friend, so I need to see the doctor.

You can't take her. She has to be discharged.

I am taking her. We've got her on a flight to South Africa and we have to leave for Bombay right now.

No, that's not possible. You heard what the policeman said, there's an investigation. You can't take her.

I want a DAMA, I say with false confidence, and I must have it right now.

You will have to wait for the doctor.

I'm not waiting. To show how serious I am, I signal to the others to get Anna out of bed. Give me the form to sign or I'll take her anyway.

Furious and steely-eyed, the nurse brings the form. I show Anna where to sign and then we hustle her through the crowded corridors to the side-entrance and the waiting taxi. At every moment I expect the venal hand of the police to close around us, and as we swing out of the hospital gates the sense of freedom is enormous. When they make the movie, I say, I want Tom Cruise to play me.

Faye Dunaway for me, Caroline says.

Even Anna joins in. Julia Roberts, she says, and we're all laughing. But the levity doesn't last long. In minutes it dawns on Anna that we're not going back to our hotel, and she starts to moan and protest. I want to go back to the beach, she cries, I want to finish my holiday. You have no right to do this. When I tell her the police will come looking for her there, she falls temporarily silent, but then she starts up again. Just give me my money-belt, give it to me. You can't have it. Give it to me and drop me at the side of the road. Fortunately she's wedged in at the back between Caroline and Paula, or she might make a break for it. Do you see what they're doing, she yells at the taxi driver, they're kidnapping me, they're criminals, they're thieves.

This taxi driver, whose name is Rex, has seen a thing or two over the last week to astonish him. He's come up to the hospital ward a few times and witnessed Anna in action, but she's setting new standards today. When we get to the clinic I ask Rex to come in with us, just in case we need an extra hand. When she sees the room where she'll be sleeping and hears that a nurse will be in the spare bed to keep watch, she goes berserk. I demand to leave right now, she shrieks, and makes a break for the door. I stand in her way and grab hold of her wrists and for half a minute we grapple silently together in a pantomimic frieze for the benefit of the open-mouthed Rex. I am, in this moment, physically afraid of her. She has power far beyond her muscular strength, there's a lunatic gleam in her eye. But she finally relents and slumps and then, once I let go, lashes out in a screaming fit, punching the walls and kicking the door, before collapsing in a howling heap on the bed.

All through the drive back to the village, Rex relives that moment. Pow, he says to himself, crash. He makes kicking, punching movements and shakes his head in wonder. It's safe to say he's never witnessed anything like it. A year or two later, out of the blue, he will send an e-mail to me in South Africa. In part it reads, how is your work going on. I hope that you may sell lots of books. I'm fine and do good business. I always remember your good words, your words are a great knowledge to me. In future if you publish a book you should write about that girl, who wished to die.

She is heavily sedated now and much calmer than she was in the government hospital. But this doesn't stop the endless stream of abuse, the accusations of failure and neglect, as well as the demands for various items. There is a telephone in the clinic where patients can make calls on credit and she rings him obsessively at the hotel, numerous times each day, with an inventory of requirements for his next visit. She wants her shoes, her money, her rucksack. He isn't willing to hand any of these over, for fear of what it might lead to, but what he can bring he does. There is never a thank you, only a litany of charges against him, which he hears out wearily. You're stealing my things, I'll have you arrested. You're so cruel and selfish. I hate you, I'll never speak to you again.

For the first time there are paid hospital attendants to watch over her and this means that he doesn't have to be there every day. He's happy to keep some distance between them. So he checks in for an hour each afternoon, then heads back to the room, but there's not much chance for rest. Instead there are frantic preparations for Anna's return. In consultation with her partner and family back home, it's been decided that she will be accompanied by Dr. Ajoy and the other friendly doctor from the hospital who helped orchestrate her escape. Arranging tickets and visas at short notice for them is a devilishly complicated business, involving faxes to the South African embassy and the airline, with all sorts of supporting documentation, some of which must come from home. But it's all finally resolved and the evening arrives when he can bring her rucksack to the hospital, along with her passport and ticket, and say goodbye.

After everything that's gone before, the moment is somehow small and empty. Her attention is not on him, but on her luggage, which she must instantly unpack and check and re-order. You see, he tells her ruefully, everything's there, nothing's been stolen. The different bags of clothes with their little labels are a sad reminder of where the journey began.

She comes outside to say goodbye. She's wearing the shoes she's been demanding for so long and appears almost serene. The high tide of madness has receded, leaving behind this translucent husk of a woman who nearly resembles his old friend. But not quite. There is a chilly reserve between them, which covers over a gulf so huge that it can perhaps never be bridged. Nevertheless, he finds it in himself to embrace her. Goodbye, he says. Take care of yourself.

You too. Enjoy the rest of your trip.

Or some such words. Whatever they say, it is in breezy phrases like these, phrases without content, or perhaps too much. Then he is driving away from her, with Rex at the wheel, looking back one last time at the solitary, lost figure in the twilight.

I t's only now that the full force of what's happened begins to hit him. Until this point he has been constantly in action, at the receiving end of calamity, with no chance for reflection. It's like a hurricane has blown through his life, flattening every structure, and in the aftermath the silence and vacancy are immense.

There is nothing to do, but his body struggles to accept it. He is constantly on edge, constantly prepared for crisis. He sleeps badly and lightly, and wakes long before dawn. The days are empty and he doesn't know how to fill them. Gradually he moves out of his head and starts to see what's around him. He notices his own face again, how much weight he's lost, the fixed stare of his eyes.

Mostly he sits around, talking to Caroline, or goes for stumbling walks on the beach. His body slows and eventually accepts the aimlessness, but inside, deep down, it's like an engine with a missing part, forever turning over, screaming in the same high gear.

News comes to him from South Africa. Anna is safely home. Then she's booked into the clinic. A great many of her friends can't or don't want to see her, they're too horrified by what she's done. At first she has tried to dismiss her stunt in India as a small upset in an otherwise wonderful holiday, but eventually acknowledges the full extent of the disaster. She's in constant touch with Jean but it's not clear where that liaison is heading.

Most of this information reaches him through Anna's girlfriend, with whom I have long tearful conversations almost every day. She continues to see Anna regularly at the hospital, even though they've agreed to separate and see what the future brings. She's in need of comfort, which I'm scarcely able to offer, and she extends comfort of her own. Sometimes she asks advice. On this score I don't hold back, let go of her, I say, she's going to kill herself one day. I know it's true, she's like a bomb that might go off at any moment and I want the space around her cleared.

All of this, the confusion and frenzy around Anna, is now on the other side of the world. He is not responsible, not accountable, any more. But of course in another way he will always be responsible for what happened and that knowledge is burned into him like a brand. At least she didn't die. He imagines what would have followed if she had and how the rest of his life would be different.

Among other things, he talks over this subject with Caroline in the weeks that follow. She is the only other player left from the drama they've just been through and they cling to each other for consolation. They keep each other company in a bickering, dependent way, almost like family. She has now become his friend, though he didn't seek her out by choice. On an arbitrary morning their lives were pushed together and fused by fate. She could have walked away when she heard me shouting, or kept her distance like the others did, and perhaps by now she wishes that she had. But instead she came up the stairs and into the room and since then she's taken up station in a corner of his life.

But this makes for a fraught and uneasy alliance, he feels he owes her a debt and at the same time resents that obligation, he wants to leave this whole experience behind, to erase every trace of it, but she's there every day to remind him. And she's carrying her own pain and loss, which have become grafted onto Anna and by extension onto him. She's in a bad state like him, not sleeping well, given to bouts of weeping. But she also seems to feel, though she doesn't say it aloud, that he's in some way a solution to her troubles, and he shrinks from that silent expectation. He has failed Anna, he will fail her too.

But his time here is drawing to a close. In just a month or two it will be unpleasantly hot, already a lot of local businesses are shutting down. He is leaving soon, meeting another friend in Bombay and travelling north, to the mountains. Caroline has tried to persuade him to stay, why don't you meet your friend, she says, and come back here. No, I tell her, I have to move on. In response she books her own ticket home for a day before his departure. This date is coming closer, and he needs it, the leave-taking, as a climax and conclusion.

On one of those last evenings, when they're eating dinner together, she says to him, what happened to me in Morocco, the accident we had there. You know, where I lost my husband.

Yes.

I haven't told the story yet. I've told some of it, just the basic facts. But the whole story, what actually happened, I've never told to anybody.

Yes, he says, and he can feel what's coming. It makes him sick to the heart, he wants to run, but he stays where he is.

I would like to tell the story just once, she says now. I want somebody to hear it, then I might be able to leave it and walk away. Do you know what I mean.

He nods, he knows exactly what she means. Whatever the story is, he knows it will be terrible and he dreads taking it on. But after what she's gone through on his behalf, how can he refuse.

They put it off till a couple of days before her departure. At her request they go down to the beach one evening. The sun is beginning to sink into the water, the clouds are full of colour. They find a place away from other people, close to a little stream and a clump of palm trees, and sit on a log. I don't know how to start, she says, I've written some of it down and I thought I might read it to you. But when she takes out her sheaf of papers it all feels wrong, too wooden and formal. Just tell me, I say, just tell me what happened.

Almost as soon as she begins to speak, she's quaking and trembling. It happened thirty years ago, but it's as if she's living it again in this moment, and it becomes like that for him too. Her story travels into him, his skin is very thin, there's no barrier between him and the world, he takes it all in. And even afterwards when he wants to get rid of it he can't do it, in the weeks that follow as he tries to leave Goa and the village behind the things that he lived through there will recur in an almost cellular way, haunting him, and Caroline's story is part of it, joined somehow to Anna, all of it One Thing. Yet what can you do with a story like this. There's no theme, no moral to be learned, except for the knowledge that lightning can strike from a clear sky one morning and take away everything you've built, everything you've counted on, leaving wreckage and no meaning behind. It can happen to anyone, it can happen to you.

H is onward journey is like an endless running away. He meets his friend in Bombay and they travel northward together. Orchha, Khajuraho. By now it's full summer and the heat on the plains is like a furnace, so they head up into the mountains, to Dharamsala, where they languish for a few weeks.

In all of this he tries to behave like an ordinary traveller, marvelling at what's around him. But he hardly ever manages to lose himself, mostly he is stuck in one place in the past. The physical world feels substanceless, like a drab dream from which he will wake up into a dirty hospital ward.

He hears from Anna a couple of times. The first e-mail reaches him a few weeks after he's left Goa. Full of misspellings and strange sentence constructions, it's a note of apology for what she's done. She says that she's left the clinic and is staying with her family in a nearby town. She doesn't tell him more about the state of her life, though he continues to hear a little from her girlfriend. He knows, for example, that she can't make up her mind about what she wants, whether to stay involved with a woman or to keep her connection with Jean. Jean is going to come to South Africa, then he isn't, then he is. Meanwhile, once she's spent this time with her family, Anna will be moving out of the house she shared with her partner and into a flat on her own.

But before this can happen she's back in the clinic again. She is still suicidal, she's still a mess. She weighs fifty-five kilograms and is starving herself. She is burning and cutting herself again. A lot of her friends still won't have contact with her, and some who do have a secret compact with death themselves. She has acquired an otherworldly halo, both attractive and repellent, she has gone beyond some fatal threshold and managed to return.

She writes again after a few weeks have passed. She's out of the clinic once more and has realized, she says, that whenever she feels suicidal she needs to get help. She sounds calmer now, more composed, or perhaps it is the flatness of depression. Jean is with her and they are touring around. We get on really well, she says, I'm delighted that he has come to visit. There seems to be a future for us as a couple. She adds that she will be going back to work in a couple of weeks and ends by saying, take care my friend and hope one day you find it in your heart to forgive me.

He doesn't reply, simply because he can't. There is no desire to punish her, any more than a means to forgive her, what happened has put them beyond that. He doesn't know why she can't see it herself. They are in a place where language has no purchase and, whatever happens, he doubts that this will change. The closest he can come to Anna is in speaking to her partner, which is how he still thinks of her, although technically she isn't that any longer. She still loves Anna very intensely, but while Jean is in town she is keeping away. He asks what will happen once Jean has gone. Will you try again with her.

I don't know, she says. I don't know what she wants. I don't think she knows herself.

Even in these conversations language will never be enough. What she's been through is a special kind of heartbreak. She has looked after Anna, taken care of her, for almost eight years and there is no doubt that without her Anna would have died long ago. Yet now she has been sidelined, shoved into the wings, by Anna herself and by others allied with her. Anna's family, who have never liked the idea of her being with a woman, have seized on this alternative future with a man and are pushing it delightedly. But I saw how it was with Jean and I know there's nothing there, no future and hardly any past.

How little future will soon be revealed to everybody. The message comes just a few days later. He has known for a while now, since she made her attempt in Goa, that she will kill herself one day, and only the time and the circumstances are uncertain, and yet when he reads the words they still hit him like a physical force that propels him backwards in his chair. Anna is dead. On the day after Jean's departure she took a massive overdose of pain-killers while she was alone in her apartment. Her sister became concerned when she didn't return phone calls and got a locksmith to open the door and found her lying on her bed.

There is more, but the words are blotted out by the fog that has filled the room, erasing time. The last two months never happened, she is sleeping on that bed in Goa, he has just seen the medicine wrappers on the floor and realized what she's done. He jumps up in shock and rushes out into the street. It's as if he has somewhere to get to, something urgent to do. He wants to call for help, he wants to grab hold of somebody passing and tell them to find the doctor, he wants to keep her alive. It takes him a moment to understand that the news is irrevocable, it cannot be undone. Not now and not ever, because the dead do not return.

Even then his journey isn't over, though in another sense it ended long ago. He considers returning to South Africa, but in truth he doesn't want to, and what would be the point. So he continues travelling, or running away, up into the high mountains, to Ladakh. He only does return home, in fact, a month or two later, when there is a genuine threat of nuclear war between Pakistan and India, and his fumbling, half-hearted exit feels like a fitting conclusion to the story.

So he is not in Cape Town to see her body laid out for viewing in an open casket, or the huge service that overflows from St. George's cathedral, all the spectacle and public grief that she so ardently wanted, and that she seemed to think she'd be around to witness. He hears about these things, of course, and they evoke a sad, angry dread in him, like the news of an earthquake on the other side of the world. But the closest he comes to her again is a silent confrontation with a bag of ash and bones, all that's left of her after the cremation. This is at her girlfriend's house, the first time he goes to visit. He stares at the bag and pokes it with his finger. Shakes his head in amazement. It seems bizarre, to the point of bitter laughter, that a human being can be reduced to this.

A couple of years later, when he's travelling in Morocco, he spends a night in Agadir and takes a taxi the next morning to a dusty hillside outside town. He has intended to buy flowers but hasn't managed to find any, so he arrives empty-handed. The day is burning hot, he hasn't slept properly the night before, he has a bad headache. You want me to wait, the taxi driver asks him. No, come back in half an hour. Is it enough time, half an hour. Yes, it should be enough.

He imagines he will easily find the spot and pay his respects and leave, but it doesn't happen as he imagines. The taxi driver has dropped him in the wrong place, so he has to walk partway down the hill. When he finds the European cemetery the gate is locked and he has to shout for somebody to let him in, and once inside he's lost. The graves spread chaotically in all directions, with no clear logic, no plan. He stumbles up and down rows of headstones, names swimming past, and more than forty-five minutes have gone by when he arrives by chance at the one he's looking for. It's all exactly as Caroline told him, the cracked slab with its inscription, its final enclosing dates. Next to it, on the left, is a nameless brown hump of earth, the grave of a woman, a friend who was killed in the same accident. Her family didn't have the means to bring her body home or to memorialize her properly.

Maybe it's only the heat, or his headache, or the tiredness, but he finds himself suddenly, unexpectedly, sobbing. He tries to stop the tears, but they keep on coming. A huge emotion is welling up in him, unattached to the scene, he doesn't know either of these people, after all, and they died a long time ago. But it seems unbearably sad that a life should come to rest here, on a sun-blasted hill above a foreign city, with the sea in the distance.

Caroline's story from the beach is with him again, memory and words inseparable from each other. But it takes him a while to realize who he's really weeping for. Lives leak into each other, the past lays claim to the present. And he feels it now, maybe for the first time, everything that went wrong, all the mess and anguish and disaster. Forgive me, my friend, I tried to hold on, but you fell, you fell.

The moment seems to drag out for hours, but it's probably only a minute or two before he pulls himself together. He feels awful, but also relieved somehow, emptied out. By now the taxi driver is hooting impatiently outside. The day is wearing on and he has a bus to catch, a journey to complete. It's time to go. He dries his eyes and picks up a tiny stone from the ground, one like millions of others all around, and slips it into his pocket as he walks towards the gate.

Acknowledgments

Thanks to Stephen Watson, Tony Peake, Nigel Maister, Ben Williams, and Marion Hänsel. My especial gratitude to Philip Gourevitch and his fine team at the *Paris Review*, where these pieces first appeared.

The quote on page 62 comes from William Faulkner.

ABOUT THE AUTHOR

Damon Galgut was born in Pretoria, South Africa in 1963. A previous novel, *The Good Doctor*, was a finalist for the Booker Prize and the Commonwealth Writer's Prize. He lives in Cape Town.

Carmine Abate
Between Two Seas
"A moving portrayal of generational continuity."
—*Kirkus*
224 pp • $14.95 • 978-1-933372-40-2

Salwa Al Neimi
The Proof of the Honey
"Al Neimi announces the end of a taboo in the Arab world:
that of *sex!*"
—*Reuters*
144 pp • $15.00 • 978-1-933372-68-6

Alberto Angela
A Day in the Life of Ancient Rome
"Fascinating and accessible."
—*Il Giornale*
392 pp • $16.00 • 978-1-933372-71-6

Muriel Barbery
The Elegance of the Hedgehog
"Gently satirical, exceptionally winning and inevitably bittersweet."
—Michael Dirda, *The Washington Post*
336 pp • $15.00 • 978-1-933372-60-0

Gourmet Rhapsody
"In the pages of this book, Barbery shows off her finest gift: lightness."
—*La Repubblica*
176 pp • $15.00 • 978-1-933372-95-2

Stefano Benni
Margherita Dolce Vita
"A modern fable...hilarious social commentary."—*People*
240 pp • $14.95 • 978-1-933372-20-4

Timeskipper
"Benni again unveils his Italian brand of magical realism."
—*Library Journal*
400 pp • $16.95 • 978-1-933372-44-0

Romano Bilenchi
The Chill
120 pp • $15.00 • 978-1-933372-90-7

Massimo Carlotto
The Goodbye Kiss
"A masterpiece of Italian noir."
—*Globe and Mail*
160 pp • $14.95 • 978-1-933372-05-1

Death's Dark Abyss
"A remarkable study of corruption and redemption."
—*Kirkus* (starred review)
160 pp • $14.95 • 978-1-933372-18-1

The Fugitive
"[Carlotto is] the reigning king of Mediterranean noir."
—*The Boston Phoenix*
176 pp • $14.95 • 978-1-933372-25-9

(with Marco Videtta)
Poisonville
"The business world as described by Carlotto and Videtta
in *Poisonville* is frightening as hell."
—*La Repubblica*
224 pp • $15.00 • 978-1-933372-91-4

Francisco Coloane
Tierra del Fuego
"Coloane is the Jack London of our times."—Alvaro Mutis
192 pp • $14.95 • 978-1-933372-63-1

Giancarlo De Cataldo
The Father and the Foreigner
"A slim but touching noir novel from one of Italy's best writers
in the genre."—*Quaderni Noir*
144 pp • $15.00 • 978-1-933372-72-3

Shashi Deshpande
The Dark Holds No Terrors
"[Deshpande is] an extremely talented storyteller."—*Hindustan Times*
272 pp • $15.00 • 978-1-933372-67-9

Helmut Dubiel
Deep In the Brain: Living with Parkinson's Disease
"A book that begs reflection."—*Die Zeit*
144 pp • $15.00 • 978-1-933372-70-9

Steve Erickson
Zeroville
"A funny, disturbing, daring and demanding novel—Erickson's best."
—*The New York Times Book Review*
352 pp • $14.95 • 978-1-933372-39-6

Elena Ferrante
The Days of Abandonment
"The raging, torrential voice of [this] author is something rare."
—*The New York Times*
192 pp • $14.95 • 978-1-933372-00-6

Troubling Love
"Ferrante's polished language belies the rawness of her imagery."
—*The New Yorker*
144 pp • $14.95 • 978-1-933372-16-7

The Lost Daughter
"So refined, almost translucent."—*The Boston Globe*
144 pp • $14.95 • 978-1-933372-42-6

Jane Gardam
Old Filth
"Old Filth belongs in the Dickensian pantheon of memorable characters."
—*The New York Times Book Review*
304 pp • $14.95 • 978-1-933372-13-6

The Queen of the Tambourine
"A truly superb and moving novel."—*The Boston Globe*
272 pp • $14.95 • 978-1-933372-36-5

The People on Privilege Hill
"Engrossing stories of hilarity and heartbreak."—*Seattle Times*
208 pp • $15.95 • 978-1-933372-56-3

The Man in the Wooden Hat
"Here is a writer who delivers the world we live in…with memorable and moving skill."—*The Boston Globe*
240 pp • $15.00 • 978-1-933372-89-1

Alicia Giménez-Bartlett
Dog Day
"Delicado and Garzón prove to be one of the more engaging sleuth teams to debut in a long time."—*The Washington Post*
320 pp • $14.95 • 978-1-933372-14-3

Prime Time Suspect
"A gripping police procedural."—*The Washington Post*
320 pp • $14.95 • 978-1-933372-31-0

Death Rites
"Petra is developing into a good cop, and her earnest efforts to assert her authority…are worth cheering."—*The New York Times*
304 pp • $16.95 • 978-1-933372-54-9

Katharina Hacker
The Have-Nots
"Hacker's prose soars."—*Publishers Weekly*
352 pp • $14.95 • 978-1-933372-41-9

www.europaeditions.com

Patrick Hamilton
Hangover Square
"Patrick Hamilton's novels are dark tunnels of misery, loneliness, deceit,
and sexual obsession."—*New York Review of Books*
336 pp • $14.95 • 978-1-933372-06-

James Hamilton-Paterson
Cooking with Fernet Branca
"Irresistible!"—*The Washington Post*
288 pp • $14.95 • 978-1-933372-01-3

Amazing Disgrace
"It's loads of fun, light and dazzling as a peacock feather."
—*New York Magazine*
352 pp • $14.95 • 978-1-933372-19-8

Rancid Pansies
"Campy comic saga about hack writer and self-styled 'culinary genius'
Gerald Samper."—*Seattle Times*
288 pp • $15.95 • 978-1-933372-62-4

Seven-Tenths: The Sea and Its Thresholds
"The kind of book that, were he alive now, Shelley might have written."
—*Charles Spawson*
416 pp • $16.00 • 978-1-933372-69-3

Alfred Hayes
The Girl on the Via Flaminia
"Immensely readable."—*The New York Times*
164 pp • $14.95 • 978-1-933372-24-2

Jean-Claude Izzo
Total Chaos
"Izzo's Marseilles is ravishing."—*Globe and Mail*
256 pp • $14.95 • 978-1-933372-04-4

Chourmo
"A bitter, sad and tender salute to a place equally impossible to love
or leave."—*Kirkus* (starred review)
256 pp • $14.95 • 978-1-933372-17-4

Solea
"[Izzo is] a talented writer who draws from the deep, dark well of noir."
—*The Washington Post*
208 pp • $14.95 • 978-1-933372-30-3

The Lost Sailors
"Izzo digs deep into what makes men weep."—*Time Out New York*
272 pp • $14.95 • 978-1-933372-35-8

A Sun for the Dying
"Beautiful, like a black sun, tragic and desperate."—*Le Point*
224 pp • $15.00 • 978-1-933372-59-4

Gail Jones
Sorry
"Jones's gift for conjuring place and mood rarely falters."
—*Times Literary Supplement*
240 pp • $15.95 • 978-1-933372-55-6

Matthew F. Jones
Boot Tracks
"A gritty action tale."—*The Philadelphia Inquirer*
208 pp • $14.95 • 978-1-933372-11-2

Ioanna Karystiani
The Jasmine Isle
"A modern Greek tragedy about love foredoomed and family life."
—*Kirkus*
288 pp • $14.95 • 978-1-933372-10-5

Swell
"Karystiani movingly pays homage to the sea and those who live from it."
—*La Repubblica*
256 pp • $15.00 • 978-1-933372-98-3

Gene Kerrigan
The Midnight Choir
"The lethal precision of his closing punches leave quite a lasting mark."
—*Entertainment Weekly*
368 pp • $14.95 • 978-1-933372-26-6

Little Criminals
"A great story...relentless and brilliant."—*Roddy Doyle*
352 pp • $16.95 • 978-1-933372-43-3

Peter Kocan
Fresh Fields
"A stark, harrowing, yet deeply courageous work of immense power and magnitude."—*Quadrant*
304 pp • $14.95 • 978-1-933372-29-7

The Treatment and the Cure
"Kocan tells this story with grace and humor."—*Publishers Weekly*
256 pp • $15.95 • 978-1-933372-45-7

www.europaeditions.com

Helmut Krausser
Eros
"Helmut Krausser has succeeded in writing a great German epochal novel."—*Focus*
352 pp • $16.95 • 978-1-933372-58-7

Amara Lakhous
Clash of Civilizations Over an Elevator in Piazza Vittorio
"Do we have an Italian Camus on our hands? Just possibly."
—*The Philadelphia Inquirer*
144 pp • $14.95 • 978-1-933372-61-7

Lia Levi
The Jewish Husband
"An exemplary tale of small lives engulfed in the vortex of history."
—*Il Messaggero*
224 pp • $15.00 • 978-1-933372-93-8

Carlo Lucarelli
Carte Blanche
"Lucarelli proves that the dark and sinister are better evoked when one opts for unadulterated grit and grime."—*The San Diego Union-Tribune*
128 pp • $14.95 • 978-1-933372-15-0

The Damned Season
"De Luca…is a man both pursuing and pursued. And that makes him one of the more interesting figures in crime fiction."
—*The Philadelphia Inquirer*
128 pp • $14.95 • 978-1-933372-27-3

Via delle Oche
"Delivers a resolution true to the series' moral relativism."—*Publishers Weekly*
160 pp • $14.95 • 978-1-933372-53-2

Edna Mazya
Love Burns
"Combines the suspense of a murder mystery with
the absurdity of a Woody Allen movie."—*Kirkus*
224 pp • $14.95 • 978-1-933372-08-2

Sélim Nassib
I Loved You for Your Voice
"Nassib spins a rhapsodic narrative out of the indissoluble
connection between two creative souls."—*Kirkus*
272 pp • $14.95 • 978-1-933372-07-5

The Palestinian Lover
"A delicate, passionate novel in which history and life
are inextricably entwined."
—*RAI Books*
192 pp • $14.95 • 978-1-933372-23-5

Amélie Nothomb
Tokyo Fiancée
"Intimate and honest...depicts perfectly a nontraditional romance."
—*Publishers Weekly*
160 pp • $15.00 • 978-1-933372-64-8

Valeria Parrella
For Grace Received
"A voice that is new, original, and decidedly unique."—*Rolling Stone* (Italy)
144 pp • $15.00 • 978-1-933372-94-5

Alessandro Piperno
The Worst Intentions
"A coruscating mixture of satire, family epic, Proustian meditation, and erotomaniacal farce."—*The New Yorker*
320 pp • $14.95 • 978-1-933372-33-4

Boualem Sansal
The German Mujahid
"Terror, doubt, revolt, guilt, and despair—a surprising range of emotions is admirably and convincingly depicted in this incredible novel."
—*L'Express* (France)
240 pp • $15.00 • 978-1-933372-92-1

Eric-Emmanuel Schmitt
The Most Beautiful Book in the World
"Eight novellas, parables on the idea of a future, filled with redeeming optimism."—*Lire Magazine*
192 pp • $15.00 • 978-1-933372-74-7

Domenico Starnone
First Execution
"Starnone's books are small theatres of action, both physical and psychological."—*L'Espresso* (Italy)
176 pp • $15.00 • 978-1-933372-66-2

Joel Stone
The Jerusalem File
"Joel Stone is a major new talent."—*Cleveland Plain Dealer*
160 pp • $15.00 • 978-1-933372-65-5

Benjamin Tammuz
Minotaur
"A novel about the expectations and compromises that humans create for themselves."—*The New York Times*
192 pp • $14.95 • 978-1-933372-02-0

Chad Taylor
Departure Lounge
"There's so much pleasure and bafflement to be derived from this thriller."
—*The Chicago Tribune*
176 pp • $14.95 • 978-1-933372-09-9

Roma Tearne
Mosquito
"Vividly rendered…Wholly satisfying."—*Kirkus*
304 pp • $16.95 • 978-1-933372-57-0

Bone China
"Tearne deftly reveals the corrosive effects of civil strife on private lives and the redemptiveness of art."—*The Guardian*
400 pp • $16.00 • 978-1-933372-75-4

Christa Wolf
One Day a Year: 1960-2000
"Remarkable!"—*The New Yorker*
640 pp • $16.95 • 978-1-933372-22-8